God's Forgotten Daughter

A Modern Midrash: What If Jesus Had Been A Woman?

KATHERINE CHRISTINE SCHNEIDER-AKER

the
WOMEN's
series

from LuraMedia

© Copyright 1992 LuraMedia
San Diego, California
International Copyright Secured.
Publisher's Catalog Number LM-636.
Printed and bound in the United States of America.

Cover image by Sara Steele.
"Phalaenopsis" ©1981 by Sara Steele, All Rights Reserved.
Cover design by Bernadette G. Littlefield.

LuraMedia
7060 Miramar Road, Suite 104
San Diego, CA 92121

Library of Congress Cataloging-in-Publication Data
Schneider-Aker, Katherine Christine, date.
    God's forgotten daughter : a modern midrash : what if Jesus
had been a woman? / Katherine christine Schneider-Aker
        p.   cm. -- (The Women's series)
    ISBN 0-931055-92-X
    1. Jesus Christ--Fiction. 2. Bible. N.T.--History of Biblical
events--Fiction.   I. Title   II. Series: Women's series (San Diego,
Calif.)
PS3569.C52315G6   1992
813'.54--dc20   92-25378
                                                        CIP

LuraMedia™

*Dedicated
to the women of the Bible
whose stories were left out
and all the women
through the years
who have shared
their stories with me.*

Acknowledgments

I wish to acknowledge all my sisters in the struggle against injustice and oppression. This story was born of my kinship with them.

Kathleen Hayden, Elaine Sinaisky, Claire Janaro, and Jo Kirkpatrick were particularly present for me during the joyful birthing process of *God's Forgotten Daughter*. My writers' collective, the Wild Women Writers, were wonderful in their ongoing love, support, nurture, and intellectual challenge and assistance during D'vorah's gestation: Betty Brooks, Christine Leigh, Elizabeth Keller, Pat Paolilli, Maryann Crosse, Rosalie Friis-Ross, Mary Miller, Judy Zdravje, Melody Fountain, and Marty Smith. Pat Reif, chair of the master's program in Feminist Spirituality at Immaculate Heart College Center, was another midwife for D'vorah, as was the Feminist Spirituality community. Rabbi Denise Eger helped clean the baby up, and Lura Jane Geiger welcomed her with open arms.

There are few women as loved and cherished as I am by my family and friends. They are with me in everything I do, and D'vorah is as much theirs as mine: my mother, Lois Rainwater; my sisters, Lisa, Shirley, Sharyn; my brothers, Franz, Stefan, Herb; my daughters, Bronwen and Lois; my aunt, Ann Scheer; my uncle, Bradley Scheer; countless nieces and nephews and greats; my granddaughters; my godmothers, Nancy Lockwood and Amanda Booth Sherlock; and so many friends: Jaime Jameson, Betsy Cancilla, Mary Gilvarry, Roberta Moore, Jane Brubaker, Norella Hyde, Renee Lancon, Levonne Kelly, Wanda Perrin, Barbara Schneyer, Hildegard Huntsman, Chris Berardo, Ruth Cairns Baker, Laurie Drabble, Alison Fuller, Ann Hayman, Joyce Pemberton, Peggy Streid, and Shelly Wiley. If I've left anyone out, I am truly sorry.

I also want to remember my father, Herbert Schneider. He would have loved D'vorah.

More than anyone else, I wish to thank my husband, Bob, who has supported me unstintingly in everything I have done, and who is as proud as any father ever was.

Introduction

At least it is remembered that we went to Calvary
with him, the other women and I, though we are
largely nameless. While the men scattered far and
wide in their confusion and fear, we were there at
the foot of the cross. Later, we were at the tomb —
for Jesus, and for ourselves. Oh, how we wept in
each other's arms in the days that followed for all
the losses of our women's lives . . . We wept until
we were empty vessels, and then we did what
women have always done: We put ourselves back
together and went about the work that was before
us to do.

God's Forgotten Daughter
Page 87

The images of the women at Jesus' crucifixion, whether watching from far away (Matthew 27:55-56, Mark 15:40-41, Luke 23:49), or at the foot of the cross (John 19:25-27), have always touched me deeply. Their courage, willingness to risk, and loyalty to Jesus throughout his life, ministry, the crucifixion, and after his death are immeasurable. It was this powerful connection between women and Jesus of Nazareth that made the idea of a full female partner for Jesus not implausible, and the idea for D'vorah as Jesus' "twin" was slowly birthed in me.

God's Forgotten Daughter is my attempt to move women into the center of sacred power, not for the purpose of *excluding* men, but for that of *including* women. *God's Forgotten Daughter* is midrash, commentary on the sacred texts, in this case New Testament gospels. I have made a point of not tampering with the story that has come down to us, but, rather, have added to it by visualizing what might have been and re-telling it as if seen through a female lens.

I believe my story is true in spirit and in form to the original, as we know it. I followed the chronology to some extent and the narrative form of the gospels. I wrote *God's Forgotten Daughter* with two versions of the Bible at hand: *The Revised English Bible*, Oxford University Press, Cambridge University Press, 1989; and *The New Revised Standard Version*, Thomas Nelson Publishers, Nashville, 1989. All biblical text has been paraphrased.

The tradition of commentary on biblical texts is long and venerable. For centuries the Hebrew Bible (Genesis through Malachi) has been interpreted and reinterpreted by Jewish biblical scholars. This process of reinterpretation is called "midrash": sermons, homilies, and fables that expand sacred texts, enriching them with voices and thoughts from different people and different historical contexts.

Christianity did not carry on the same tradition of midrash, though there are oral and cultural traditions that have attached themselves to the New Testament, and contemporary scholars sometimes use the term to describe what they are doing with the texts. These interpretations and reinterpretations, though not written out in the same way as Jewish midrashim, have the same power as lenses through which we read the texts.

For instance, in the Roman Catholic tradition, established at various historic councils, Mary, the mother of Jesus, remained virgin all her life, having no other children. In some Protestant traditions, an understanding developed that Mary and Joseph went on to have their own children after Jesus. These are the brothers referred to in Luke 8:19. This tradition is a kind of midrash, in that it comments on the texts, and expands and enriches them with details not found in the originals. *God's Forgotten Daughter* is an imaginative re-telling of the Jesus story from the Gospels of Matthew, Mark, Luke, and John.

God's Forgotten Daughter, though not classic midrash, could fairly be called Christian midrash, women-focused midrash, or feminist midrash. It was written in much the same spirit as Virginia Woolf's "Shakespeare's Sister" in her talk "A Room of One's Own." The telling of God's Forgotten Daughter is not meant to take anything away from the story of Jesus' birth, ministry, and death, but, rather, to add other voices and sensibilities to those that have been culled from what actually happened and are handed down to us in Christian tradition.

The stories in God's Forgotten Daughter, which include accounts of violence against women and children, alcoholism, incest, battering, murder, and suicide, reflect my perception of human behavior, now and in Jesus' lifetime. I do not believe that we are more violent now or that our social, familial problems are much different from those of people throughout time. In many of the stories of the Bible can be seen remnants of stories not dissimilar to the ones I have created, and the injunctions against various kinds of behavior are even more telling.

Judith Plaskow, eminent Jewish feminist theologian, presents the idea that those who hold power in a culture can be identified in the following way: 1) Who is in charge? 2) Who does the naming? 3) Whose symbol system is being used?

In the commonly known and accepted history and interpretation of the Bible, the responses to these questions follow this sequence: 1) Men are in charge; God is a man; 2) Men, from Adam on, do the naming; 3) The symbol system is patriarchal and hierarchical. Because God is male and the only child of God is a son, patriarchal practice, the religious and secular systems under which most of us live today, is justified by a male-centered theology.[1]

---

[1] Lecture notes, Feminist Spirituality 595a, "Introduction to Jewish Feminist Spirituality," Judith Plaskow, Ph.D., Immaculate Heart College Center, Los Angeles, CA, July 24-28, 1989.

It is not by accident that the perpetrators in my stories are mostly men, nor do I consider it unfair or sexist. I deeply believe that the construction of patriarchy as a hierarchical model leads inevitably to violence against those who are perceived as lesser or other. Modern statistics on violence bear out my conclusions, and many of the biblical stories, when stripped of the softening effect of an accepting, largely unquestioning tradition, contain not only violence by men against women and children, but horizontal violence by women against other women and children in the name of patriarchy.

It is possible to read biblical stories as if outside the tradition. The rape of Dinah, Genesis 34:1-4, is an example of men becoming violent against other men, using women as the excuse. Is anyone really concerned about Dinah? Can the story of Lot's daughters in Genesis 19:30-38 be read as a story of incest of the father against his daughters? As for horizontal violence, a male-identified Sarah has Hagar, the mother of Ishmael, cast out by Abraham (Genesis 21:8-21), and the patriarchal God supports her action. Not much has changed.

The women's stories I have created are a synopsis and distillation of many of the stories I have heard in women's groups through the years. Though my stories are made up, "fiction," I believe they are in essence true and truly reflective of women's lives. It is my hope that through them women can come to feel that each of us is in charge of her own story and cannot continue to be excluded from history; that we must and have a right to name our female reality; and that through telling our stories we will create a symbol system that reverences and redeems our existence and those of all the many beings on our planet.

When I first began seriously reading the Bible, I was amazed over and over at the distance the Church has come — physically, theologically, and spiritually — from the Jesus story found in the Synoptic Gospels (Matthew, Mark, and Luke). I was also dismayed. The Jesus who spent time with the woman at the well and the Jesus hanging on the cross in many churches today wearing bishop's robes, seemed unconnected to me. I would like to have known the one, but not the other.

It was this struggle with who Jesus was — and reading and re-reading the stories, especially of his contacts with women — that eventually led me to write *God's Forgotten Daughter*. Perhaps, I thought, though I cannot separate Jesus enough from the tradition to feel close to him, I could relate to a woman, without the distortions and attachments of two thousand years of encoded patriarchal tradition. As it happens, I was right: During the entire time I was re-working Jesus' story as D'vorah's, I felt closer to Jesus than I ever had before. I still do.

— Katherine Christine Schneider-Aker

God's Forgotten
Daughter

CHAPTER ONE

I was the oldest. Our mother always told the story the same way:

"D'vorah, you were born first, and then Jesus."

It was fast, she said, not much time between us, but I was certainly the older.

The story was repeated so often that Jesus and I knew it by heart. Being twins was unusual enough, without having been born in a stable in Bethlehem, so it was not a story that we were always happy to hear. Even so, it was told over and over.

Mother said it was actually not as bad as it sounded.

"We were warm, with the big animals, cows and goats, mostly, and a donkey, in stalls around us, a few sleepy chickens in the straw, and doves overhead in the rafters. We were as comfortable as could be," she said, "with blankets and straw for a bed. You were so tiny," she told us, "I put you in one of the mangers. It was just the right fit."

The people whose barn it was felt terrible the next morning, when they learned Mother had had two babies while they slept comfortably in their beds.

"But there was really no help for it," Mother said. "The town was overcrowded for the taking of the census."

Mother always explained that she blamed no one.

"After all, everything turned out right, didn't it? Aren't you two of the most beautiful and perfect children?"

I wondered, after I became a grown woman myself, what it must have been like for her. She and my father were alone, far from their people, when their babies were born. Was she afraid? Did my father comfort her and smooth her forehead? Did she have to tell him how to help her? She never talked about her feelings when she told the story, just that we were born late at night, far from home, among strangers. And I never thought to ask until it was too late.

My first memories are of my father's shop. I am still transported there whenever I smell fresh-sawed wood. My brother and I played among the curls the plane made from the planks, with blocks of yellow and brown wood. The two of us were always together then, in my father's shop next to our house. We learned to walk there and to be careful of the tools, which were sharp and heavy.

Our father never treated us differently, one from the other. I suppose it must have made his work more difficult, having two babies under foot. Even so, I don't recall that he was ever impatient or sharp with us, unless we were in danger of some sort. It must have been a help for our mother, who was expecting another baby, to have the two of us occupied so many hours of the day. She fetched us into the house for meals and naps and baths, but our waking hours were spent mostly in the shop.

When we were a little over a year old, the new baby was born. How different it was from our birth. When my mother began to labor, we were taken to stay with a neighbor, while our house slowly filled up with women. I don't know where the men went. They all seemed to disappear from the village, and the world became female. I was included in many birthings when I was older, and the same thing always happened. Birth belongs to women.

Other things were the women's, too. The work of the world is clearly divided into men's work and women's work, I found, as the years passed and I was required to spend more and more time with Mother and the women, while Jesus spent more time with Father and the men of the village. I tended the babies, as they came. I learned to help with the bread-making and the preparation of meals, and I went with Mother to the well, where the women gathered to draw water and to talk. My mother would visit while I played with the other little girls. By then I had no wooden blocks, but rather dolls, like the other girls. No one ever asked me which I preferred.

My brother began to work in the shop alongside our father. I learned to weave at the loom in the house while he learned to make tables and chairs. Our mother taught me the lighting of the Shabbat candles, and my brother learned the recitation over the Pesach meal. My brother and father went to the small synagogue while my mother and I stayed home, and I learned to cook meals for the Holy Days of our year. My brother learned to chant the prayers with the other men. I learned embroidery and mended and decorated the prayer shawls.

CHAPTER TWO

I was told that I walked first and talked first. When we were little, we were the same height and size, but I was aware of my responsibilities as the older twin, from the oft-repeated story of our birth, so I looked out for my brother as if I were bigger. Later, of course, Jesus grew taller than I did, though he was never a big man, certainly not as big as Peter, but I remained his big sister. Some things cannot be changed.

I was short, like my mother, and I looked like her, I was told. Pretty, people told me, with my mother's dark eyes and straight, brown hair, the same hair my brother had, and the same dark eyes. I had a friend, Rachael, who had curls and a hint of red in her hair. I always wanted curls and a hint of red, but my hair was straight and brown as the mud of the river banks. It seems unimportant now that I am old, my hair gray from grief and age, but when I was young, the longing to be like Rachael hurt me to my bones.

From what I saw in the families around us, my brother and I were unusually close. Perhaps it was because we were twins. Other brothers and sisters fought when they played, but we never did. And our little sisters and brothers went as quickly to Jesus as to me when they were frightened or hurt and our mother was not in the house. In fact, he had more patience with them than I did.

Our lives began to diverge more and more as he became a man and I became a woman, but something between us held us together. He always told me about the synagogue, describing the old men and the ceremonies, chanting the prayers for me over and over until I even learned some of them. Women didn't have to go to synagogue, and we usually didn't because there was so much else to do.

Jesus even made up his own prayers, he told me, and he taught me some of them. I don't think he was supposed to make up prayers, but he said that the words just came to him sometimes, like words to lullabies for the babies came to me, or stories. I liked his prayers, their sounds and words, and I sometimes chanted them softly to myself as I walked with some of the little ones to market or took meals to one of my other brothers who worked in the fields. My mother often looked at me, her gaze clear and focused, when I chanted Jesus' prayers as I cleaned or prepared meals, but she never said anything to me, so I never stopped.

CHAPTER THREE

When we were nearly twelve, Jesus and I both began to dream quite often, and the dreams were eerily similar. We talked together about them, seeming to know, the way children know things, that we could not tell anyone else. Our mother, who was not afraid of anyone or anything, would have been frightened by the dreams: the shadowy crosses, the dying men, the weeping women, the black tomb. We also dreamed of angels, shining with the same bright soft silver light of a summer moon. The angels always told us not to be afraid, and after a time we weren't, even though we grew to know, deeply in our hearts, that one of the dying men was my brother.

But most of the time we were just children, working by our parents' sides, helping with the little ones, playing with the other children. We learned, too, the stories of our people. My brother loved the stories of the prophets the most, and I loved the story of Miriam leading her people in song. We both loved the story of Moses parting the Red Sea and drowning the Egyptians, for we were an occupied people, prisoners of the Romans as surely as Moses' people had been of the Egyptians, even though we were on our ancestral land.

Our father told us we were of King David's line and that David had danced on the steps of The Temple in Jerusalem. It made us feel special, knowing that we were descended from the great King of Israel, even though we knew our people had lost most of their power. My brother heard talk among the men that the Messiah would return one day and Israel would be restored. It was just a matter of time, he told me.

Our family was large. Mother's parents were dead, but her cousin Elizabeth, though ancient, still lived not far from us. My father's mother lived with us until she died, and I remember her as a sharp old woman with a soft spot only for my brother. She died when we were about six, and it was a relief to me, though my father cried. We had lots of cousins and other relatives, near and far, but the one we liked best was Elizabeth's son, John.

John was different from all the rest of us, even as a child, and I know that's why Jesus and I liked him. He was wild, though not cruel. He hated to be confined and often slept on the roof of his house, even when the nights were cold. He went to school with the other boys, but he learned the prayers faster and chanted louder than any of the others. The only one who was not embarrassed by him was my brother, who told me that John should have lived in the Age of the Prophets.

I liked John because there was something pure about him, something untouched and clean and clear. He scared all the other girls, but he never scared me, and I often walked with John and my brother and listened to them talk.

All they ever talked about was the coming of the Messiah, and they argued endlessly over what the world would be like afterward. Jesus said that the Messiah would bring peace, not war. I honestly didn't know where he got such ideas, but it gave me something to think about. John said that the Messiah would restore the land to the people of Israel, that the Romans would be cast out. He said the Messiah would sit on the throne of the Great King David, and Israel would never more be subservient to pagans and goddess worshipers.

It was as if the two of them understood the Unnameable in different ways, and yet my brother, later when he began to preach, used some of John's violent images. Perhaps he knew by then that the people understood war much better than they could a peace they had never known.

CHAPTER FOUR

We learned in quite a strange way that we were healers, and we kept it secret for many years. We must have been about nine the first time. We were playing by ourselves near the river. I don't know why we had no babies to watch that day, but we didn't.

Mother had to have been washing our clothes or we never would have been allowed so close to the water. Jesus and I were making a palace in the mud when Rachael came running up to us. Her foot slipped in the mud, and she fell on the rocks at the water's edge. She did not get up, and my brother and I moved as one toward her.

We told each other later that it was as if we were propelled by something outside ourselves, a huge hand pushing us gently toward Rachael. We were not frightened. We did not scream for our mother or run away; instead, we went to Rachael, who was lying face down in the water and had a great bleeding gash in her temple.

Jesus lifted her from the water and turned her over. Her face, with gore all down one side, was as pale as death, and her open eyes were blank. My brother wrapped his arms around her and began to chant one of the men's prayers, or perhaps it was one of his own. I put one of my hands over the wound in Rachael's head and the other over her staring eyes. Power arced around us. The bleeding stopped, and Rachael's eyes closed gently.

Jesus held her for a few more moments as we watched the color return to her face. I used the hem of my skirt to wash the blood off her. The wound had closed. Rachael opened her eyes.

"What happened?" she asked.

"You fell," my brother told her. "D'vorah and I pulled you from the water."

He released her and she sat up. The wound was fading, and the blood in the water was rapidly washing away.

"Are you all right?" I asked her, though I could see for myself that she was.

"Just a little dizzy, D'vorah. Thank you for rescuing me."

We helped her up, and she was wobbly at first, but by the time we delivered her to her mother, she seemed her usual self, if somewhat damp and subdued. There was no sign of injury.

That night, after we were in our beds, my brother and I talked about the healing. Our experience was identical. The power entered us, even before we got to Rachael, and when we touched her, we felt the power pass through us into Rachael. It had never happened to us before, yet we both knew what it was and how to use it. We knew that the power had come through us *both*, though we learned later that we did not have to be together to heal. We also learned later what a dangerous gift it was.

CHAPTER FIVE

W hen Jesus and I were twelve, our family went up to Jerusalem, as we did every year, to celebrate the Passover. It was our favorite Holy Day, happy and filled with good food, not like Yom Kippur, a sad and serious day of fasting, which we would have to observe now that we were grown. And we liked Jerusalem, with its traffic and noise and smells and sights, as unlike our home as could be.

Usually we looked forward to the visit, but, for the first time, Jesus and I were to be completely separated. Since we were no longer children, Mother explained to us that we must abide by custom and The Law and honor our separate roles in life.

Jesus seemed to take it pretty well. After all, he got to do the interesting things: go to The Temple, read from the Holy Books, be where the men were, while I got to do what I would have been doing at home anyway: cooking, cleaning, and serving the men. Even though we had our own special women's section in The Temple, if we had time to go there, it really made me furious, especially as Jesus seemed to take no notice of how shut out the women were from everything that was really holy. And he seemed not to care that, except at communal meals and the Seder, we would be apart.

After a time I calmed down. There wasn't much else I could do. But I told myself that some things needed changing and that I would be the one to change them. I didn't know then how change threatens those in power and to what ends they will go to retain power and retaliate against any who attempt to instigate change. It was a lesson I would learn and relearn all the rest of my life.

At any rate, I was so angry with Jesus that I vowed to avoid him all the way home. We were traveling in a rather large band for safety, so this seemed easily accomplished. I just stayed with the women, but as each hour passed and Jesus did not come to find me, my heart broke a little more. Finally, I was feeling so hurt and neglected that I decided to find him and tell him exactly what I thought of his abandonment of me.

By the time I realized that he was not traveling with us, I was really frightened. It was not unknown for children to be kidnapped and sold into slavery. That certainly was a threat all our parents used to control us during travel, and I had no reason to believe it was not true.

With tears running down my face, I ran to my father and threw myself into his arms, babbling incoherently about slaves and bandits and kidnappers. The men he was walking with smirked a little at the sight of a daughter bringing so much attention on herself, but Father took care of that with an unusually stern look.

When he finally got the gist of what I was trying to report, that Jesus was not with our group, he grew very still and serious.

"Take me to your mother, D'vorah," he said. "Nothing can be done without talking it over with her."

Well, Mother was enormously upset, though she controlled it very well. I have always thought of her as very strong and filled with courage. Just the story of our birth showed that. On that day, and in the future, I would learn just how strong she really was.

With very little hesitation we decided to go back to Jerusalem by ourselves, on the chance that Jesus had been left behind. We gave the little children and babies to some neighbors who were traveling with us to take home. They simply added the extra children to their own. I didn't think until much later how unusual it was that I, a girl, was included on that return trip to Jerusalem. I should really have been left to help care for the little ones.

I thought nothing of it at the time because I was so agitated. I expect my parents knew of my upset and suspected that I would be of more use solving this mystery than going home knowing nothing. Perhaps they even knew a little of the many ways Jesus and I were connected. Regardless, they took me with them, and when we finally found my twin talking with the men in The Temple, none of us knew whether we were glad or mad.

Jesus felt terrible when he realized what had happened. He'd simply lost track of time, like anybody involved in something interesting, but he had never gotten in trouble before, and this was pretty big trouble. He could see in our eyes all the dire thoughts we'd had before seeing him alive and well. Even more, he and I both knew, from our dreams, that we would cause our parents graver pain than this in the future, which may have been why we always tried so hard not to upset them.

CHAPTER SIX

By then, we were so late that we had to spend another night in Jerusalem, Mother worrying about her babies and Father wondering whether and how to punish his eldest son. The curled and gray-bearded Rabbis Jesus had spent the lost time with were very impressed with him, and they told my father so. Jesus seemed as impressed with them as they were with him. I think that's when he decided to become a Rabbi himself.

We all went to bed early, my parents exhausted with worry and relief. Lying on a pallet across from me, Jesus whispered about the fascinating conversations he'd had with the Holy Men, but their words seemed to have very little to do with our real lives, and I told him so.

My remark launched another of our endless discussions on what was more important — life as we lived it day to day, with its troubles and joys, or the idea of the new world to be founded at the coming of the Messiah. These discussions had been going on between us for several months, and our opinions were coming closer together.

We had started at very different places. Jesus believed that the coming of the Messiah would overthrow everything that was now in place, but he was a little sketchy on exactly what that meant. He didn't agree with John's vision of a military campaign because he believed that would simply replace what existed with more of the same. He felt the Messiah would bring peace and somehow change the order of things so that life would be better.

I, on the other hand, was very worried that those who were overlooked now would be overlooked in the coming world.

"What about the poor, the sick, the possessed?" I asked my brother. "What will the Messiah's coming mean to them? Will they be brought up in the world, will all of them be healed, will they be freed from their demons?"

"I think you may have some good questions," he answered me. "What good is it to change things if things are not fundamentally changed?" he asked himself and me.

"Fundamentally, indeed," I said, pleased that he had listened to me. None of the other boys did.

"And what about women?" I pursued.

"What about them?" He sounded startled, and I could picture how his face looked in the dark — open and puzzled.

"Well, the men never listen to them, and the women always have to stay at home with the children. Religion is really only for the men. Don't you think that the Messiah, if he truly wants to change things, should create a religion that includes women?"

I have to admit that I scared myself a little asking that question. I hadn't really thought about it as much as I probably should have. Everyone knew that the religious readings were kept from the women because women could contaminate them. We were all unclean a great part of our lives, monthly and after childbirth, while men were unclean very seldom. I wasn't sure that the Messiah, whoever he would be, wouldn't think we were unclean, too.

Nevertheless, Jesus leaned over so I could see him and looked straight at me after I asked my questions. His eyes were not shocked, but thoughtful and kind. I waited to see what he would say.

"Those may be very good questions, D'vorah. Perhaps the Messiah will really bring about a changed world by raising up the poor, curing the ill, banishing demons, and having women participate in religious matters. Perhaps those are some of the things of peace that he will put in place, in a world where no one is better than any other, female or male, poor or rich, and all are given what they need to live full, healthy lives. That certainly would be different."

Now utterly worn out, we said goodnight and fell asleep. When we got underway in the morning, our father told Jesus there would be no punishment. It was a relief to us both.

CHAPTER SEVEN

W e were pretty sure, for many years, that no one knew about the healing power we had. After Rachael, we had agreed never to seek out people to heal, but situations came up now and again when we were compelled, just as we had been the first time, to act.

We healed one of Jesus' friends, for instance. He was a very rowdy boy who one day fell out of the tree he had been climbing. As we were walking by, we could hear the snap of the big bone in his leg. No one else was around, and the same huge hand that had pushed us toward the drowned Rachael pushed us now from the path toward where David lay, broken and silent.

It was much like the first episode. David was as if asleep or dead, from the pain, I thought, and the shock. We could clearly see the unnatural bend in the leg and the blood from where the broken bone end pierced the flesh. His face was colorless, his mouth slack.

It was a wonder to me, thinking about it later, that neither of us felt the least bit sick or scared. We simply knelt calmly in the dust on opposite sides of the fallen boy. The day was hot, and the tree did not give much shade. The heat pressed down on us.

I held David's head, while Jesus placed his hands gently on the bend and the wound. We felt the power pass through us and between us into him. I felt the shock leave David like a sigh, and Jesus told me later that he felt the bone actually move back in place, though he had put no pressure on it.

By the time David opened his eyes, he had only a bruise where the injury had occurred. He seemed glad to see Jesus, but embarrassed to see me. I moved back from him as quickly as I could. It was unseemly for me to be holding him so, especially once he was awake.

"What happened?" he asked Jesus, turning away from me.

"You fell," Jesus said. "We were afraid you had hurt yourself, but it seems you haven't."

The bruise was nearly gone, leaving a dim yellow splotch on David's leg.

"You worried for nothing, Jesus," David said. "This tree's so puny, there would be no way I could hurt myself falling from it. Now, the big olive tree over near your house, well, that would be a different story."

I couldn't stop myself from snorting at his arrogance. This caused him to glance briefly my way, but he didn't really see me. I knew by then that most men didn't ever really look at women, at least in public, though I hadn't puzzled out why not. It seemed part fear and part dislike, but more than that I could not say. My father and my brothers were the only men I knew who looked women directly in the eye when talking with them. I wondered why other men never did.

Jesus and I still believed that we needed to be together to heal, that the power relied in some way on the two of us. We did healings as they presented themselves to us — a spider bite that made my friend Tamar very ill, a dangerously deep cut our brother James got while shearing sheep. We never drew attention to ourselves, and all the healings seemed comfortably convenient to those involved, but we knew we could not keep this mysterious power secret forever. There would be a circumstance in which witnesses would see what we had done, or the person healed would not accept our glib explanations of what had happened, somewhat altered from the reality.

We also did not talk to each other about the healings very much. I think we both were a little afraid of what we could do, though there was never any fear when we were healing. As Jesus' education progressed, he ascribed the power to YHWH, but I was not so sure.

I had already seen the healing the women of my village did among themselves, using herbs and potions. Though not all of their remedies worked, they sometimes healed women of child-bed fever and often of their monthly pain. I had seen them dry up the milk of a mother whose baby was born dead so that her suffering would not be prolonged by the reminder of the futile flow. They lanced boils and drew the poison out with packs of curing herbs. They brought down the fever of a child with a rich, healing broth. I even heard them claim to have made fertile a barren woman and to have stopped another woman from being able to conceive after she nearly died in childbirth several times. I never knew if all these stories were true, but I had no reason to doubt them.

CHAPTER EIGHT

Before I was very old, I knew that within the world of men existed another world of women and, though the women knew a lot about the world of men, the men knew very little about the world of women. This was the world where women cared for and helped each other, with their skill and their talk and their presence. It was the world in which unhappy wives gained the strength to continue in marriages they could not leave. It was the world in which daughters could rail against the unfairness or brutality of their fathers without fear of dangerous consequences. It was the world where women, who seemed invisible to the men of their families, villages, and larger communites, could be seen, by other women. It was where we valued each other's work and worth. It was what made most of our lives bearable and, on occasion, joyful.

Perhaps Jesus, alone of all the men, knew about the women's world. Partly this was because he and I were so close that our lives were not totally separate, like most sisters' and brothers'. Partly it was because I told him about it. But I believe that it was more because of some difference in Jesus himself, the same difference that allowed him to hear what I had to say about women.

Whatever it was, he was able to be present in the women's world in ways other men could not be. With all the other men, the women's conversations abruptly ended as soon as one of them entered the doorway. It would not have been right for women to discuss their problems in front of men. Those topics were left for times when the men were gone from the house, and the women would gather to talk while they worked so that the time passed more quickly.

Not so with Jesus. He would often sit and work with us while we sewed or cleaned and prepared food, listening as female

problems were discussed: painful menstruation, difficult preg-
nancies, the horrors and dangers of childbirth, problems with
marriages or with children, the tensions of families that were too
large in houses that were too small, the often thankless care of
elderly relatives.

The women never seemed to notice Jesus was there or to
think about the fact that he was a man. They never once looked
up suddenly, embarrassed to discover him amongst them. Later,
during his ministry, this easy familiar way with women puzzled
the twelve. Until his death, and even after, women were his truest
allies and friends. For most of them, he was the one man who
would look them in the eye.

CHAPTER NINE

I was the one to discover that we did not need to be together to heal. I was visiting my friend Miriam, who had been ill for a very long time. No one seemed to know what was wrong with her; she just faded and failed a little every day, as those who loved her stood by helpless.

I tried to visit her regularly and to be cheerful when I did, for her sake. She, I believed, tried to be cheerful for me, too, and for her other friends and her parents and brothers and sisters. Though she surely knew she was dying, we never spoke of it until this surprising visit.

I must have looked shocked when I saw her, so much had she failed since last I'd seen her. Her face mirrored my own for a moment before she held out her arms to me and began to cry. I went to her and, sitting gently on her pallet, held her to me and rocked her as I would have rocked one of the babies at home.

I hoped only to comfort her, as she cried and clung to me, but something else began to happen that I could not account for right away. I began to see a dim image, something in Miriam's head that I could feel did not belong. To see it better, I closed my eyes. In my mind it became more clear. I felt it pushing, silent and unseen, inside Miriam's head on whatever it was that helped her live and walk and move, crushing the very life out of her. It seemed to have an evil life of its own, growing and growing, until my friend would die and it would die with her.

Her sobs began calming. She was probably tiring. I could feel the energy ebbing from her in waves. I needed to do something before she was entirely calm again, and I shifted her weight onto one arm so I had a hand free. This I surreptitiously placed on her head, over where the thing was growing. I could feel the power leap out of my hand. It arced around and through the awful thing. Then, gradually, I could feel it begin to shrink, and, as Miriam quieted in my arms, she did not push me away, but lay still and restful against me.

In a few moments I knew that the growth would continue to shrink until it disappeared entirely, and Miriam would eventually be well. I moved my hand to a more natural position, and Miriam sat back against her pillows. Already her color was better. It would take months for her to return entirely to herself, to regain the weight she had lost and learn to walk again, but I knew it would happen. No one would ever know what had made her ill or what had made her better, but it did not matter.

We visited for a little while. Then she told me she needed to sleep. I left her with a sense of gladness growing in my heart. Miriam would live.

CHAPTER TEN

Our cousin John began making a name for himself baptizing men in the River Jordan. He did this with fiery preachments about being cleansed of sin and with quotes from the Prophet Isaiah. As always, Jesus and I were curious about John's actions. An unusual child of aged parents, he had become an even more unusual man, and our close friendship with him did not cease with the end of childhood.

Of course, I could no longer go wandering about with Jesus and John as I had done, so I learned to be mostly satisfied with the lengthy stories Jesus brought back to me. Jesus told me that some were saying that John was the Messiah, which John adamantly denied. Jesus and I conjectured over whether John really could be the Messiah and eventually decided that it was not possible. However, we did hear that he was preaching more about sharing one's worldly goods than of conquering the enemies of Israel, and I wondered if perhaps the talks Jesus and John and I still had about the nature of the new world had anything to do with this.

Jesus told me that he was still spending as much time with John as he could, when he was not needed in our father's shop. They talked about much the same things Jesus and I talked about, and John eventually told Jesus that he thought perhaps Jesus was the One to come. Jesus, of course, had a great laugh over the absurdity of that, but it was cut short, he told me, by the utter seriousness of John's countenance.

Jesus heard him say, "Someone more powerful than I am is coming. I could not even tie his sandals for him."

Jesus told me all this with a sort of amazed look on his face. We were together in our father's shop alone. I was sweeping, and Jesus was finishing some fence posts for a neighbor. It was so familiar to be in that place that we were reminded for a moment about how young we had been such a short time ago. Both of us were still having the same dreams, and we were increasingly feeling that time had speeded up. When we spoke of time passing, our parents assured us that it always passed more swiftly as one grew up, but Jesus and I knew there was more to our feeling than was natural.

We grew to speculating about why John felt Jesus might be the Messiah. We had continued healing but believed that only we two knew about it, even though we both knew it could not be kept secret much longer. We were certain John didn't know about it, so that couldn't be why. Jesus had completed his training and become a Rabbi. He even preached locally now and then, but he was not very different from the many itinerant preachers who came through the area from time to time. In fact, there was little to distinguish Jesus from any other young male, as he kept his more radical ideas pretty much to private conversations with those he knew well. He feared that the concept of the new world, formulated in the many talks with me and with John, would bring him notoriety he preferred to avoid.

So, whatever John saw in Jesus remained a mystery to the two of us. We did manage to laugh somewhat ruefully at the idea of John unfastening anyone's sandals — John, who never even wore sandals himself.

The story of Jesus' baptism by John was one of my favorites because it illustrated very clearly the shift in the cousins' relationship to each other. Jesus should have gone unnoticed in the general baptism of ten or fifteen other men who waded into the Jordan at John's side. However, according to John, the breath, the spirit of YHWH, was with them as Jesus emerged from the river, dripping wet, his beard shining with droplets. John knew then that Jesus was the Chosen One.

"It was as if," he told us both later, awe still in his eyes whenever he looked at my brother, "I heard the voice of the Lord."

CHAPTER ELEVEN

After the baptism Jesus spent some time alone in the desert. He never did tell me exactly what happened there. I believed then, and still believe, that he needed to spend some time by himself to consider his life and his work. What I do know is that when my brother came back, he seemed to have made up his mind about something.

I could hardly wait to be alone with him, but when he returned to us he was exhausted and dirty and weak with hunger. My mother hurried around trying to do everything at once for her eldest son, who over his lifetime had been so little trouble to her. I, alone, seemed to notice that he came back a different man from the one who had left us. It frightened and worried me. Did this mean that he and I had changed in relationship to each other?

We were nearing our thirtieth birthday when Jesus came back from the desert. Neither of us had married, though I had been expected to. There had been some effort to keep Jesus and me apart for a while in the idea that we would never seek out spouses while we had each other. This failed to make either of us more interested in eligible suitors, so the plan had eventually been abandoned, to the great relief of everyone involved.

Meanwhile, I was feeling more and more unsettled in my role of helper to my mother. It was not that I disliked my duties. Indeed, I loved helping with the children, weaving, cooking, and all the rest. Mother and I were very close, and I knew my help was appreciated. We had all seen women go to early graves from overwork, but my mother had a youthful countenance, even though she was nearly forty-six.

It was just that I had this feeling that I was not where I belonged, that my life would not stay on this steady course it had followed for all these years. Where I would go or what I would do remained as much a mystery to me as the healing power, which continued to grow with the years, as if knowing how greatly it would be needed.

After Jesus had been back from the desert several days, we arranged to spend some time alone together. Jesus announced to the family that he and I needed to talk, as if marking off our time from regular time. He had never done this before. We had always managed to find time for our conversations within the structure of our daily lives: sitting together on the roof before we went to bed, working in the shop, walking through the village for one purpose or another.

My parents' response puzzled me as much as Jesus' announcement did. They asked not one question, but my father, after exchanging a significant look with my mother, retired to his shop, while my mother said she would take the little ones over to Jael's to help her with carding the wool from her family's sheep.

When we were alone, I burst forth with all the questions that had been simmering.

"Where were you? What has happened to you? You've changed. What is going on?"

Jesus smiled at me, his face still so eerily similar to mine. Peculiarly, I realized that he was no longer a boy, but was a man of middle years, while I was a woman past marriage. It gave me pause as I thought briefly about the children I would never have.

"Where I have been is not important," Jesus said, over my objections that it was. "I am not sure myself where I have been. Part of it was trance, and some of it I only dreamed, I know. But, when I woke, I knew suddenly what it was I need to do now, and you are a part of it."

"Me?" I asked, not comprehending what he could possibly mean.

"Yes, you, D'vorah. What we are meant to do is to go out through the land and preach about the new world that is to come, the world in which all people will be free."

"But, Jesus, I am a woman. I can't preach."

"Maybe you can't preach to the men, as you couldn't be baptized by John. I'll preach to the men. But you can talk with the women, who don't even have to know what you are doing. You can carry our message to some of those who need it most."

Well, it was such an enormous idea that I could not take it in all at once. I was certain I could do it. In fact, deep inside I was sure that this was what I had been waiting for, but it would so set me outside the community as I knew it that I was not sure I wanted to do it. What risks it would involve! How different I would be, not in the invisible way the healing made me, but in front of everyone I knew, and strangers too.

"What do you think, D'vorah? You are so much a part of me that I don't think I can do it without you."

Those were the magic words. How could I not do it?

We spent some days getting ready to leave our home and go out into the world. We told our parents why we had to leave. Again, there was no protest, only that sharp, aware look passing between them, as if they had known all along we would do this. Neither my mother nor my father spoke against my traveling alone with my brother. In fact, in every way they stood by us and, by their every action, let us know that what we did had merit with them. The day that we embraced them as we departed, we both tried to tell them how much they meant to us. They said it was not necessary to say and told us to go and be well.

CHAPTER TWELVE

W e lived in a time of much illness. Death was all around us, as Jesus and I knew better than anyone. We had many cures between us over the years, but we had kept the power close to ourselves, fearing the consequences should it become public knowledge. As we moved out into the world, Jesus felt we should heal in clear sight at our first opportunity.

I was not so certain that was what we should do. After all, preaching and healing were two different things. We could not predict how our preaching would be received, but we were pretty certain that healing in public would attract much attention, and not necessarily the right kind. Even so, Jesus was adamant.

"I am sure that is what we are to do," he said.

I didn't ask him how he knew. He seemed so certain that it hardly mattered.

And so we began our work. Jesus and I went out into the countryside while awaiting our chance. He preached to the men, and I helped the women feed the people who followed us. While the women and I worked, we talked. It was like the usual talk, except that sooner or later it would veer around to what my brother was saying to the men. I would say it to the women, but in my own words.

"Jesus believes that when the Messiah comes, the order of things as we know it is going to be overthrown." So far this jibed with what they had heard all their lives.

"We believe that the Messiah will raise up the poor and bring down the rich. We believe that he will raise up women and children, and free slaves." I always got their attention with that. "We believe that in the Kingdom all will be equal in the sight of YHWH, who will bless us all. Cripples will walk, women will no longer suffer in childbirth, the deaf will hear, no baby will die as it is born, the dumb will speak, the blind will see, and the mad will be made whole. All the people of the earth will love one another and the God who made them."

Each group we spoke to was different. Sometimes we so displeased our hearers that we needed to move on rather quickly. Other times, no one wished us to leave ever, and it was at those times that our vision of the future blazed clear and bright before us.

This went on for some days. We spent each night with strangers who quickly became friends, and we walked abroad during the day. We did not fear robbers or other criminals, believing ourselves to be about the Lord's work. Each evening we talked over all that had happened during the day, how we had been received, who had liked what we were saying and who had not. It was no surprise that the rich and the educated, those whose privilege was a fence around them, disagreed with us, and on more than one occasion we were threatened with violence. The poor, however, could not hear too many of our words. Only the women continued to be an unknown factor, and I learned how frightened most women were of the men they lived with: fathers, fathers-in-law, husbands, and sons.

It would usually begin in the same way. We would reach a small community or family group, and Jesus would make it known that he was a Rabbi prepared to preach to the people. He would acknowledge me as his sister, traveling with him, which raised eyebrows more than once. However, as I quickly found my place with the women, I was not long considered a problem.

People would begin to gather, the men around Jesus, the women around me, with their children and the responsibility for feeding the men. Jesus would begin preaching, using the familiar approach to his insurgent point of view. Away from the men, perhaps at the back of the crowd or in someone's house, I would talk with the women and eventually put our message before them.

Often they were shocked, both by what I had to say and because I felt free to speak for my brother. Had they known that some of what we had to say originated with me, how much more shocked they would have been. Many times I was hushed, as the women glanced around fearfully to see if I had been overheard. Sometimes I was able to get them to talk about their fears, assuring them that I would not betray them.

Every time I was stopped from speaking a message I felt to be full of hope, my heart broke for my sisters. I wanted them to hear me joyfully, for I promised them freedom and worth and stature, but too often their terror caused me to cease talking, and after an awkward moment, they would pick up safer strands of conversation, glancing anxiously my way from time to time.

Jesus and I spoke much of this in the evenings, as we also talked of the men's fear of change and loss of power in the world to come. It had seemed to us that our ideas, hammered out in discussion after discussion between Jesus and me, and Jesus and John, would have been embraced heartily by people whose lives were so hard and harsh. We had spent so much time talking about the inequities of the world in which we lived, so much time trying to envision redress and justice, so much time listening for Wisdom, that we could not see what we were doing wrong.

But, from this many years later, as I think again of those tentative beginnings, it becomes abundantly clear what we were doing wrong: We were offering a world they could not see or understand, so different was it from what they knew. We were promising them things that we believed in, but that most people had never had the will or the time to consider. What was so self-evident to us was only unknown to them, and thus they were afraid. We were simply speaking in a language they couldn't understand, so they couldn't hear what we were saying.

CHAPTER THIRTEEN

We reached Capernaum in Galilee late one midweek afternoon. As we always did, we went to the synagogue so Jesus could announce himself, in the hopes of gaining an audience and a place to spend the night. As Jesus went in the front entrance, I waited in the courtyard, where the sellers of sacrificial animals sat by their cages of birds, holding kids on tethers. It seemed very peaceful to me. I was looking around for a place to sit and rest when a madman entered screaming Jesus' name.

"Why are you here, Jesus of Nazareth? Have you come to kill us?"

I hurried to where the man stood before the great door. Gently, I put my hand on his arm. He turned to me.

"I know who you are, too, Daughter of the Most High."

His voice crackled and his eyes were wild, careening to me and back to the empty doorway, skidding across the sellers, who had backed up against the walls of the courtyard, dragging the little goats with them.

I grabbed his arm more firmly, just as Jesus appeared and came toward us.

"Be quiet," Jesus said to the demon in the man, his voice ringing in the courtyard, and I felt that part of the man fall silent. "Come out, demon," he said, and the man collapsed like falling bricks.

Jesus and I knelt on either side of him, as we had done so long ago when David had fallen out of the tree. But this was another time and another place. We were in a strange city, and people we did not know were gathering around us.

My hand, which had partially broken the man's fall, was still on his arm. I could feel that he would be recovered and back to himself in moments.

"He's fine," I said in a low voice to my brother.

"Yes," Jesus said, and our eyes met over the body of the man.

Without needing speech, we spoke to each other, "Now it is done. Now they know what we can do and who we are. Our lives will never be the same from this moment on."

We reached our free hands across the man, who was waking up, and briefly clasped them together. It would be nearly the last private moment we were to know.

CHAPTER FOURTEEN

The news spread, and Jesus was the talk of the whole district. He preached to larger and larger crowds, while the women and I managed larger and larger meals. Even so, it was the beginning of a good time. Both of us were where we felt we should be. In our different ways, to our different audiences, we were spreading the news of a new world, a different way of life, a better way than any of us had ever known. And the people needing healing now came to us.

The first was Simon's mother-in-law, ill and delirious with a dangerously high fever. Together, we cast the fever out of her. Others followed with diseases of all kinds. Though we now knew that we could use our voices to order demons and disease to leave the bodies they plagued, we still put our hands on those we could touch. It helped us to understand the deep troubles people had, to contact the darkness within them, to touch them. We, who had led an easy life, albeit unusual, who had known health and love, who had parents to cherish us, brothers and sisters to care for us, a community to keep us safe, rapidly grew in knowledge of the horrors that can be the human state. They never failed to move us and to cause us to value even more the good news of the Kingdom to come. We believed in our vision and knew that we must do whatever we could to bring it about.

Jesus preached in the synagogues of Judea, while I helped the women with their work. I held babies drooling with the cutting of teeth, and they stopped fussing and fell asleep. I comforted young mothers who had lost their babies in infancy, or childbirth, or miscarriage. I could not take away their grief, but I could leave them strong and well. Once I held an old grandmother to ease her passing from this life. Her daughters thanked me again and again for the end of her suffering.

As I was taken into the families by the women, I learned of their joys as well as the deep sorrows of their lives. I celebrated the public things: the births of healthy children, birthdays, marriages. I celebrated the private things, clapped with happy mothers when their babies took the first step, spoke the first word. I gathered with the other women when one of the girls began to bleed, becoming a woman. I found that the women circumvented the punitive laws against them by celebrating the very changes the men believed made them unclean. They created of their ostracism a time of renewal, a female time to be glad of their priceless life-creating capacity. All of this made me more glad than ever to be a woman, and some of the lifelong envy of Jesus and John that I harbored deep within slowly left, leaving me lighter and more at ease with who I was.

As the crowds following Jesus grew, so did the tales of his powers. We sometimes had a good laugh together over the stories during our before-bedtime talks, which we still had when we could. At other times we wept at the people's need for miracles to make the poverty of their lives more bearable. Yet we understood it, because everywhere we went we encountered deep, endless pain and want.

Some of it we already knew: illness and early death, injuries and lingering death, the ugliness of leprosy, the fear of madness, and all the women's diseases. We knew about hunger and poverty, taxes no one could pay, laborers ill-treated by their employers, beggars begging from people with nothing to give, while even the dogs of the rich had their fill every day. What we hadn't known about were the secrets within families that were kept from the community, and it was these hidden things I began bringing to Jesus from my hours with the women.

I brought him the story of the baby girl whose mother I had been with during the baby's burial. The baby had bled to death after being raped by her father.

I brought him the story of the child hidden at the back of the house, misshapen, malnourished, driven half mad by isolation and terror, tied up and regularly beaten by a father who was drunk all the time. The mother, paralyzed by her own terror, had only let me see the little boy after being assured I would not let the father know that she had. Forbidden to intervene in what was happening, I left the boy peacefully asleep. He would not draw his father's attention that night and by morning he would be dead. It was all I could give the child.

I brought Jesus the story of the mother so despondent after the birth of her first child that she took her own life. Her young husband blamed the baby. The woman's family blamed the husband, who eventually went mad from grief and shame and killed his mother-in-law, his child, and then himself.

I brought Jesus the stories of these forgotten wives and children, the families broken and in pain, and we started to see and understand the actual depth of healing the world needed. We knew it was beyond our gifts, and we often doubted ourselves and our cause. But we struggled against the doubt, hoping only that wherever our healing came from, there was more, even enough somehow, for all the hurting people everywhere.

CHAPTER FIFTEEN

Jesus had begun to draw the attention of the powerful, the scribes and Pharisees. As we had feared, they did not like what he said or what he did. Jesus was criticized for breaking bread with tax collectors, and for the fact that many of his followers did not fast and pray, as the followers of John and the Pharisees themselves did.

"The sick need a doctor, not the healthy," he told them. They did not understand.

He was also criticized for breaking the Sabbath. When charged with healing on the Sabbath, he said, "I ask you: Is it permitted to do good or ill on the Sabbath, to save life or to let it go?"

He might as well have been talking to himself. I saw their faces, the misunderstanding, the fear and confusion. Jesus was not making friends among the powerful and rich. I was glad I was a woman and unworthy of attention.

I remember when Jesus and I first realized that healing took power from us. We were on our way to Jairus' house to see his daughter, who was ill unto death. Somehow we got separated in the crowd, which happened more and more. I was told by someone who knew me that there was a woman in the crowd who had suffered a flow of blood for twelve years and wished to come to me so I could heal her. But my women and I were pushed to the back of the throng, and she, too, was lost somewhere in the masses.

Women often sought me out instead of Jesus, for they found it more comfortable to approach me than him, not knowing of his special way with women. I was usually easier found, too, being often at a slight distance from the multitude that followed my brother. Later, Jesus told me that the woman with the flow of blood did find him and, though she was embarrassed, touched the hem of his robe and was healed. He felt the power go out of him into her. It was the first time he felt the cost, and we learned that our power was not infinite.

For some time there had been people traveling with us. From among them, Jesus picked his disciples, the twelve men who would play such a vital role in our future. I suppose you could have said that I had disciples, too, but the women and I never formalized our relationship the way the men did.

The man closest to Jesus was Simon Peter. We were both fond of this burly fisherman with the great heart. I believe that Peter loved Jesus as much as I did, though he didn't seem to understand Jesus very much. I suppose it is a great gift of love to be so loyal to an enigma. If that is so, none of the twelve loved Jesus half so well as Peter.

Peter's wife and son came with him and joined the contingent of women I found around me. Esther was a slight, shy woman with pale eyes, pale hair, and fair skin. She and Peter had a bond between them that was deep and intense. Without questioning, she left her home to go with her husband to follow an itinerant Rabbi who was preaching an inflammatory message of liberation and equality. Never once did she appear to question her choice, or Peter's. In her own way she was as sturdy as her husband, and as loyal to me as he was to my brother.

Some of the other disciples brought their wives along, too. James' wife, Ruth, was a wonder with the children, though she herself remained childless. It was something she grieved every month, and something I was not able to change. My gift had limits, I learned. Philip's wife, Joanna, was somewhat older, more my age. Her sharp way with words caused some problems among the women, and we got a lot of exercise practicing peace. Even so, because she was a very strong woman, she was a great help in establishing camp as we traveled the countryside.

Thomas' wife, Sarah, was a singer and a storyteller. After the crowds had dispersed in the evenings, and the camp settled down in the quiet under the starry arch of sky, she would tell stories of our people and sing King David's songs. Sometimes she would lead the women in singing, as Miriam had done. Other times she would sing her own mournful songs of exile, reminding each of us that we had left our homes and safety for what sometimes seemed a dream.

Jesus and I were finding new ways of describing our vision, of making ourselves understood. We learned the value of story-telling from Sarah and began making up our own stories, or creating them from scenes we had witnessed and other stories we had heard.

I loved to hear Jesus use women and women's work in his parables. No other Rabbi ever thought to do that. He compared the Kingdom of the Lord to yeast that a woman mixed with flour until it was leavened.

He talked about the lost souls of Israel by comparing them to a coin. "Or what woman having some silver coins, does not light a lamp if she loses one of them, sweep and search the house carefully until she finds it? When she has found it, doesn't she rejoice to have found the coin that was lost? Just so, I tell you, the Lord feels joy over one sinner who repents."

Jesus amazed some by describing the world to come as a place where no one would go hungry, where those who wept would laugh, where no one would be left out, where the people would dance for joy. He said, "I tell you to love your enemies, do good to those who hate you, bless those who curse you, and pray for those who abuse you. If someone strikes you on the cheek, turn the other, and if someone takes away your coat, do not keep back your shirt. Give to everyone who begs, and if anyone takes away your belongings, do not ask for them back. Do unto others as you would have them do unto you."

This was a vision nearly beyond comprehension, and the community had many long talks around the dying fire about how it would be possible to live in such a way. Jesus and I rapidly admitted that we did not know how to live this way either, only that people must somehow learn or the world would be lost. So we practiced together as a small community. On most days we did not do very well. But now and again we would rise to the vision, we would live with each other in peace and love, and our hope would be renewed.

CHAPTER SIXTEEN

In Capernaum we were invited to sit at table with one of the Pharisees. That is, Jesus was invited. I went along, as I always did, to join the women of the house in talk and work.

An unusual incident happened while the men were at table, one I would always remember. A woman from town, a prostitute of the streets, came in to Jesus, crying and carrying a small flask of oil. She was not well kept, as the street women invariably are not, despised as they are. All the secrets she knew about the men who used her were etched in her face. She might once have been pretty and had to be quite young, as prostitutes did not live to be old. But her face was mostly hidden under the dark blanket of her hair, which fell below her waist.

I was in the room when she came in the front door. Knowing she did not belong there, she kept her face ducked down, her body crouched against any threat. The Pharisee and his other guests, all well-known, powerful men, moved as if to rise to their feet, but Jesus signaled them to be still. The woman shuffled cautiously but steadily toward Jesus, scanning the other men through her dirty hair. I could feel the link between her and Jesus already forming. This was another kind of power that was growing in Jesus and me, the power to connect with the lost and lowly. Jesus stayed very still, waiting, as the tableau formed.

When the woman reached my brother, she knelt before him. She was crying silently. Her face was wet with tears. She opened the flask, removed Jesus' sandals, and anointed his feet with oil. I could smell the myrrh from where I stood, completely caught up in what was before me. I wondered what kind of sacrifices and degradation she had suffered to acquire a thing of such worth.

When Jesus' feet were wet with oil and tears, the kneeling

woman wiped them with her hair. It did not seem to matter that it was dirty and matted. While she cleaned my brother's feet, her hair shone with cleanliness and health.

When she was done, my brother rose and brought her to her feet, holding her hands in his. Her head was still down, her face hidden. He lifted up her face with his hand under her chin. Her eyes went to his, and they stood that way, looking at each other, for a long time. The Pharisee and his guests had not dared to move again, but they glanced meaningfully at each other, believing, perhaps, that Jesus himself was mad.

Everyone jumped at the sound of Jesus' voice in the still room.

"Your sins are forgiven and your suffering is over," he said to the woman. "Go now and be peaceful. Your faith has made you whole."

Before our eyes, the woman straightened and stood tall, brought her head all the way up, and with one hand pushed her hair over her shoulder. The link between her and Jesus broke, but she kept some of the power of it in her. Without another word, she left the room.

I met her again many years later, after Jesus' death, when we were still trying to work out what it all meant. She told me that no man had ever looked at her the way Jesus had, touched her as he had, with respect for her person. Her own father had started her on the path she had taken, substituting her for her mother at her mother's death, then casting her from her home when she had become pregnant. Until Jesus touched her, she had only waited for the painful, ugly death she knew must come, of disease or violence or neglect.

"He touched something in me I didn't know I had," she told me, "something good and strong, something that hadn't been destroyed by my father or any of the other men.

"It was barely alive in me, when he touched me, but after that it grew, and as it grew, chances came to me to change the way I lived. I took them all, and today I live with a kind and gentle woman. We work together weaving beautiful things, for which the wives and daughters of the very Pharisees at table that long ago day pay me well."

I have never tired of the stories, many similar to hers, that people tell me, right up to this day, about the man my brother became, especially the stories of women. How many of them there are, from such a short span of time. How much good he did, even as time was beginning to run out.

CHAPTER SEVENTEEN

With so many of us living in such close quarters, personal relationships were sometimes very complicated. Even so, a number of babies were born during the three years we were together.

I was the midwife, and my helper was Mary of Magdala. Jesus had brought her into our family group. She told me that she had been inhabited by demons, which Jesus had cast out.

Mary was not quite pretty, but her face was so alive, her eyes so bright and quick, that one never noticed. She was about my height, a little heavier, with very delicate hands, and almost-black hair and eyes. Her voice was deep, and she spoke slowly, choosing her words carefully.

Mary had been abandoned as a child by her mother and had never known her father. She had been raised in her village with little care and no love, kept barely alive eating leftover food and wearing leftover clothing. I sometimes wondered, as I learned her story, if her demons were not named abandonment, neglect, ignorance, poverty, starvation, brutality, and shame. If so, many other people carried at least some of them.

She had gifts very close to mine, but her gifts seemed to have made her life even harder. What was for Jesus and me a healing power turned into a hurtful power for Mary because she was denied the use of it. So often we saw those whose intelligence had died because it was not nourished, whose compassion had been stillborn in the face of hatred, whose passion for life had been turned into a longing for death that they sometimes accomplished. Mary seemed to be one of those people. But when her demons left her, she began to blossom and to reclaim her birthright.

Mary worked many nights at my side in the community and the nearby villages to bring another life safely into the world. While we were together, we often talked about the nature of this world and our hope for the new world. Our talk seemed to soothe women in labor, especially as we assured them that in the promised future they would suffer no more, but bring babes into the world with joy and gladness.

We also talked about Jesus. It was apparent to me and to the other women that Mary loved Jesus, and Jesus loved Mary. In fact, next to myself and Peter, Mary was the one to be seen with Jesus the most. Perhaps in another world, in another life, it would have been granted to them to marry and bear children and live to be old together. In this life, with time swiftly passing, it had to be enough for her to hear all about him from me, and then to spend what time with him she could. If she ever resented the cup given her to drink, I never heard her say it.

I don't exactly remember when we heard that Herod had put John into prison. Many stories were about at the time concerning what it meant, and briefly the idea that John was the Messiah was revived but quickly died when John did not manage his own release.

We wanted to visit him in prison, but Jesus was warned by one of the twelve that his own life might be in danger as well as John's. My brother did not want to acknowledge this, but Peter and I managed to convince him that he would be wiser to stay clear of Herod. When John was later executed in such a terrible way, we were sorry we had not taken the risk.

Jesus aged after John's death. The life we were living, always on the move, often among strangers, sometimes hungry and cold, aged us all. From time to time our vision dimmed, and we came very close to going home on several occasions. But something always happened to pull us back from that decision and to set us firmly on our path once again. More than once, it was the kindness of strangers and the unexpected bounty people provided that restored us.

For instance, it was becoming more and more difficult to feed the crowds that followed Jesus. Occasionally, the tension this created nearly caused schism within our ranks, setting the women, who were expected to feed everyone, against the men, who said it was not their job to feed people. Sometimes our community existed for days in a kind of chilly silence over the problem of food. But each time Jesus and I were ready to intervene, out of the crowd would come food, and plenty of it. We never really understood how it happened. We knew food did not just appear, but whether it came from those who had been hoarding and had a change of heart, or new people joining us, we knew enough to offer up hearty thanks and to eat our fill while we could.

CHAPTER EIGHTEEN

Mary of Magdala shared some of our gifts. She also shared our dream of death. When she came to me early one morning with tears coursing down her face, I already knew why. It was time to go to Jerusalem to meet whatever was there. Knowing there was nothing to do, we held each other for a long while, crying. As the members of the community awoke, they passed around us, doing morning things, in utter silence. All of us knew that Jerusalem meant the end.

But the trip was far and we would not hurry. We stopped in every village, sensing that our chances to share the vision were fast passing away. Despite our feeling of urgency, we took care to spend as much time as seemed needed.

Jesus and I were not the only ones preaching anymore. Mary of Magdala had begun witnessing, using her own story to tell our larger truth. Women who once would have thrown stones at her on the street, mistaking her demons for her, welcomed her into their homes and listened to her story as if their lives depended on it. They, too, knew demons and longed to be free of them in the new life ahead.

In one village we recruited two sisters, as unlike each other as could be. Mary, the younger, was quiet and contemplative, while her older sister, Martha, took charge of everything, and woe to any who got in her way. Unfortunately, her own sister frequently did not move fast enough to suit her, so often came in for lecturing.

Martha even shamed her before Jesus, or tried to. Jesus cleared up the matter in no time, helping Martha to understand that different did not mean wrong, just different. It took her many years to really understand what he was trying tell her, but she was willing to wrestle with it, and the sisters were important through all of what was to come.

In another village Jesus incurred the wrath of the president of the synagogue for healing on the Sabbath, an old sin with him, had the president only known. Jesus healed a woman bent over double for eighteen years. When she stood straight before him and he looked her in the eye, he told me later, he knew for just a moment that it would all be worth it, all of it. Sometimes now I think of that and wonder if he may still be proven right.

Jesus did more and more preaching, using his storytelling techniques to make his points ever more effectively. Still, many did not understand him, and I questioned, to myself, why they continued to flock to him in such huge numbers. Was it that they were in such need? Was it something about Jesus? It was obvious to me that even the disciples didn't really comprehend him, yet they were as loyal as they'd ever been, doing as he asked, living this life that was no life for anyone with any sense.

I was still telling my story, too, and I believed many of the women understood me quite well. I tried to stay with what I knew, to tell my story truthfully, and to tell the stories of the women who had touched my life. The women who listened to me knew these stories, or some like them, from their own experience, and each one who grasped the vision was free to tell her own story to others. I began to picture a delicate spider's web of women's stories, woven, interwoven, and connected all across the land, each woman's story a crucial strand in making the thing whole. It was an image I carried with me through the last days.

CHAPTER NINETEEN

Jesus and I had not had a chance to talk for many months, except in passing. Both of us were busy with the work of our growing community. Being always on the move took its toll in exhaustion, and sometimes some of us lost hope. The most important things, we found, were seeing that all were well rested and, whenever possible, well fed. Everything depended on these basics.

It is true that we had lots of help with the work. The disciples — especially Peter, his loyalty unswerving — kept morale high by expressing their ongoing belief in Jesus' work. They also protected Jesus and the rest of us from those who wanted to hurt us, for whatever reason. We brought a message that was as disturbing to some as it was comforting to others, and we learned to be alert to subtle changes in the moods of individuals, small groups, and crowds.

Jesus came to me one night after we had decided to move toward Jerusalem and asked me to walk with him. It was a cool, spring night so I dressed warmly, all the while wondering what this special singling out meant.

Jesus had grown to fit the place people set aside for him. In the three years we had been traveling, he, who had started out young and unfinished, filled with grand, half-thought out ideas, had become a mature man. For some time I had admired his new stature, while still missing the Jesus who had been particularly mine. It had cost me to see him move out into the world alone, going about his work with such fearlessness and purpose. I missed him, the brother who was so much a part of me, especially our talks at night before going to bed, at the very time I was proudest of who he had become. So this summons, if that's what it was, was welcome but unexpected.

We left the camp by ourselves. I surmised that the twelve had been admonished not to follow him, as was their wont. We talked about ordinary things at first: the people who traveled with us, disputes that had been settled or still festered, children who were growing up, women and men who had recently joined us. When we were out of sight of the campfires and out of hearing, we sat silently together on a big boulder and looked, for a time, at the sparkling sky.

"D'vorah," Jesus broke the silence, "we will soon be going up to Jerusalem, and I do not know when, or if, we will get the chance to talk again."

"I've missed you, Jesus," I said simply. I could feel tears behind my eyes, and the stars I was gazing at blurred.

"I've missed you, too, D'vorah," he said as he put an arm around me. For a time we stayed that way. He kept his arm around my shoulders, and I leaned gratefully on him, who had always been my home.

"All that we know is soon to end," Jesus said, his tone thoughtful. I kept silent. "The community will change when I am gone." I didn't protest. What was the point? We had known this for a very long time. "Instead of our vision, they will develop their own."

"They'll credit you, you know, for everything they do," I spoke softly, matching his thoughtfulness.

"Yes, they probably will. I suppose it's no use trying to explain to them that there is no need, that they must take responsibility upon themselves for what they do and what they believe."

We were quiet again.

"Do you think we have done what we needed to do, D'vorah?"

I was surprised at his question. It had been a long time since he had shown any doubt. Had this been there all along?

"I'm not sure what you mean," I answered truthfully. "What was it we needed to do?"

"To talk about a better way, to show people that there is no reason to live in such poverty and want. To convince the rich that their money must be redistributed, so that no one has too little or too much. To plant seeds of hope where only hopelessness now grows." He paused.

"We've done that, Jesus. But if you're asking me if we have convinced anyone, well, I don't know. We have seen many rich men give up their wealth, and I suppose that we will see more do it. But most of the rich won't, you know, give up what they have. They don't see it as being too much, and they surely don't see those who do without as being worthy of sharing their wealth. So, my answer, in part, is that we have carried the word. I don't see that we can do more than that. We are only human."

"They believe I am the Messiah, you know."

"Yes, I know. They have great need of a Messiah, and you are so good. You listen to them, you care about them, all of them. You do not flinch from anyone.

"You even spent time with that Samaritan woman," I went on, remembering the incident clearly. It had caused such controversy among the twelve. "You weren't bothered by her in any way, who she was, how many times she had been married, none of it. Do you wonder that she thinks you are the Messiah? No one ever listened to her, spoke to her as you did. You must have heard what Peter and the rest had to say about it. They were horrified. 'What will people think?' was all they could say. Have you ever asked yourself, 'What will people think?' "

He turned to me and hugged me to him, laughing.

"Of course I have asked myself that, D'vorah." He laughed louder. It was so good to hear him laugh. "I ask myself every day. It's just that she was such an interesting person. I've heard many interesting stories from people I'd least have expected. If I didn't listen to someone because he was a Samaritan or a Canaanite, or whatever, even a woman," he laughed again, "think what I would have missed! There is too little time. I can't afford to ignore anyone." His voice grew serious and, I thought, a little sad.

"Do you think you are the Messiah, Jesus?"

"Sometimes," he answered truthfully. "Just the power to heal makes me wonder if it might be true. But, then, I tell myself, you also have the power to heal, and no one ever mistakes you for the Messiah."

It was my turn to laugh, and I laughed long and hard, Jesus' deep voice joining me as soon as he realized what he had said. We laughed and laughed until we finally wore out.

"Perhaps that is how the real Messiah will be recognized," I finally choked out. "There will be two of them, a woman and a man, and from that time onward no person shall be over any other person, and we will all be equal in the sight of the Lord and in each other's sight as well."

"Yes," I could hear that Jesus was thoughtful again, "perhaps that is how the true Messiah will become known. But, D'vorah," he turned to me with some urgency, "how can we know that we are right? How can I go up to Jerusalem to face what I have to face, being so unsure? Do we really know that life as we would have it be will be better? Do we even know there is anything after all this?" He swept his arm wide, including everything as far as the eye could see. "How can we promise people who are suffering so awfully that there will be an end, that they will someday have the things they need, the things they deserve, and be happy? How can we tell them these things if we are not sure ourselves that they are true?"

His voice was filled with anguish, and I admit I was surprised again. These were the same doubts we had had when we were young, when we had first spoken of these matters, known we were healers, and first dreamed the terrible dream about Jesus' death. Though I still had many doubtful moments, I thought Jesus had somehow moved beyond, that he was privy to some surety I was not. It seemed we were still twins in so many ways. I put my arms around him as if he were my little brother.

"Ah, Jesus. How many times I have asked myself the same questions. How many times I have faltered in the midst of telling women whose lives hold only drudgery and pain, stumbled over my own doubt. Time and again I have had to re-evaluate everything I said, everything I did."

"And what was it you found out?" His voice seemed calmer.

"I found out there is no way to know if what we say is actually true. We do not know if there is any world after this or if it is better. Those who have gone before have not returned, so we are left with our doubts. But what we do know is that the world we speak of, the world we envision and preach, is a better world, even if it does not exist. It is a better world, and if we can create it with our thoughts and with our words, if we can explain it to others, and if only one person believes it besides ourselves, then we can help make it so. And, if not us, then maybe some of the children, or their children. So long as the vision is alive in somebody's heart, it is true and as real as if we lived in it today."

Tears were streaming down my face. Without ever having put it into words before, I had said what I really believed. Jesus pulled me to him, and we clung together. He was crying, too, and, as we had laughed together only a moment before, then we cried. We cried for all the people we had helped and who could not be helped, and for all the courageous people who had listened to us and who believed with us that there was more to living than struggling, suffering, and dying. And we cried for ourselves, for lives lived as truly as we knew how, but which would soon be changed forever. And when we were through crying, we walked silently back to camp with our arms around each other. It was the last time I saw Jesus alone.

CHAPTER TWENTY

W e had agreed that not all of us would go up to Jerusalem, for there was no use in it. Some of us had not been home in the three years we had been traveling the countryside, and this seemed the best time to send people away, while the rest of us faced what waited for us.

Peter's wife, Esther, left with her older son and the two babies she had borne while we sojourned, to stay with her parents. They had not yet seen the little ones, so the pain of separation was mitigated by the idea of reunion.

Joanna wished to stay with us, and we felt that she would be an asset, given her strength and her acid tongue. Sarah, our storyteller, went to stay with her sister, while Martha and Mary returned to their home. James' wife, Ruth, took their children back to the village where she was born. The partings were sad, but we knew they were necessary. Mary of Magdala stayed with me and Joanna, while all the men left but the twelve, who would accompany us to the city.

As we were completing final arrangements in order to leave the next day, our mother arrived, much to our surprise, accompanied by a couple of young men from the village. We greeted her with gladness and confusion.

"Mother, what are you doing here?" Jesus asked her after we had embraced.

"It is time for me to join you. I knew I would arrive before you went up. I couldn't let your father come. He is too old to journey this far. So, I came myself."

"But, Mother, why? And why now?"

As she looked at him, her eldest son, her eyes were bright

with the tears she was holding back.

"Jesus, I know the dream you and D'vorah have been having since childhood. I had it before the two of you were born. Because of it, I have tried to love you as much in your lifetime as I could, to make up for the time we will be apart."

She turned to me. Escaping tears flowed over her dark, wrinkled skin.

"And, D'vorah, though you will surely outlive me, I have tried to love you enough to help you through the trials ahead. You see, I, too, know what will happen in Jerusalem, and I need to be there."

There was really nothing more to say. We embraced again, then got back to our preparations.

We began the ascent to Jerusalem the next day at dawn. The weather was hot and the road crowded and dry. We didn't have much to say to each other, though the word of Jesus' coming had spread and people lined the way, putting down palm fronds to try to quell the dust we stirred in passing. The crowds were excited, but I thought how little this journey resembled our joyful, noisy moves of the past. Their shouts only served to emphasize our silence, which no one seemed to notice. When we arrived, we split up to stay in the city with friends who knew we were coming. My mother came with Mary of Magdala and me.

Jesus grew more and more reckless over the days we spent in Jerusalem, preaching our vision publicly and challenging the Pharisees directly. Even the disciples gave him grief, questioning what rewards they would have in the Kingdom, while Jesus continued to heal publicly, to preach in parables, to count tax collectors among his friends. One day, in a rage, he even drove the traders from The Temple.

I never found out what went through his mind during those last days of his life. He seemed, when we were together, to be frenzied, as if fearing he would not accomplish what he must. He spent more and more time with the twelve and less and less time with me and the other women, even Mary. Later I believed he deliberately distanced himself from us, hoping to save us from public attention.

It never seemed to occur to Jesus, as it had begun to occur to me, that he could be moving forward into something preventable. He never considered that another outcome was possible, that he could run away, that he and Mary could still go someplace safe, marry, have children, and be happy. Instead, he faced the future head on, walking straight toward the prediction cast by his own dreams.

The town was in a great uproar, preparing for Passover, and we made arrangements to hold our Seder in the upper room of the house of a friend. When the sun set on the Holy Day of celebration, many of our people from the city and Martha and Mary joined us to share in this annual reliving of our history.

We all knew the story well. It had been part of our lives from the beginning. The houses of the firstborn sons of Israel were passed over by death, which took the firstborn sons of the Egyptians. It was one of the many Miracles of the Exile, and we loved hearing how our people had been spared. It seemed especially dear to us now, for we were, in a way, coming to the end of our own exile.

Everyone knew this part of our lives would soon be over. We could sense the future break that would forever split past from present. Even so, though the meal should have been somber, it was not.

We all were there — the women, children, and men — and the need to celebrate bubbled up in us like a spring in the desert. We had managed to live mostly at peace with one another under the most difficult circumstances for three years. We had been joined by many who shared our vision and made it possible for us to continue. We had created in this imperfect world a good effort and had lived as close to the vision we carried as we were able.

We had healed many and touched many lives. Each one of

us had grown in meaningful ways. We had been willing to risk everything for what we believed, and on the night of Passover, we gathered to celebrate our vision of a world without suffering, without injustice, without poverty, without inequality. We gathered to celebrate Jesus, who would soon be gone from our midst, and ourselves. Instead of shedding tears, we laughed and talked, and for a brief while we pushed back the darkness that was closing in on us.

When the last of the wine had been poured and drunk, and the last of the food eaten, Jesus left to spend some time with the twelve. My mother and I stayed with the women to clean up and to get what comfort we could from each other's presence.

The next days were filled with confusion and chaos for the remnant of the community abiding in Jerusalem. We first heard about Jesus' arrest from Mary, who heard it in the marketplace. All the information we got from then on came through gossip, as rumor chased rumor through the vendors' stalls. We didn't know where the disciples were, so we made do, even though the rumors were contradictory and incomplete.

Judas Iscariot, we learned, had betrayed Jesus to the Romans for a few pieces of silver. The news stabbed through the heart of the community like a dagger of ice. We could not understand it. Judas had been there from the start. He had walked the dusty roads with us, fasted and feasted with us. He had loved Jesus and carried and taught our vision. His betrayal was beyond comprehension.

We received word of Jesus' sentence late the night before he was to be crucified. We didn't believe it right away, didn't dare to believe that this was what we had all been moving toward. Was this what the years of living without a home, without the comfort of family, would amount to? Were all our efforts and hopes to end at the foot of a Roman cross? Only I, out of all the community, did not question or resist: My dreams had become reality. Eventually, the sentence was confirmed, and, feeling numb and sick, we came together to prepare.

CHAPTER TWENTY-ONE

W e rose very early, myself, my mother, Mary of Magdala, Martha and Mary, Joanna, and some of the women from the community in Jerusalem, and walked up the hill Golgotha until we were stopped by a Roman guard. Even at a distance, we could see as they nailed Jesus and two other men to huge crosses, then laboriously hoisted the crosses to an upright position and planted them in the ground.

We stayed there together, weeping, talking, and holding each other. We tried to pay attention to what happened, to manage our agony so that we could clearly remember and tell the story, if we ever needed to, tell the truth about what occurred there on that day.

It was hardest at the time for my mother and Mary of Magdala. My mother kept saying, "I never got to say good-bye, never got to tell him I love him."

I tried to comfort her, but her litany went on. There is no comforting such grief.

I have never seen so much suffering. The men hung suspended from their crosses, their arms pulled taut with the weight of their bodies. Blood flowed from the wounds in their hands and feet. I longed to take on some of Jesus' pain, to share this as we had shared so much else, but he had gone beyond me.

Mother stood next to me, and I needed to steady her from time to time; Mary was on my other side. We formed a triptych of grief: mother, sister, friend. The fact of our helplessness washed over us again and again as the day wore slowly away. At some point they pierced Jesus' side, perhaps to speed his dying. Even the Roman soldiers didn't enjoy the slow, agonizing death by crucifixion.

Jesus died about noon. I thought the skies darkened as I felt his essence leave, and my heart was rent in two. I think he spoke just before he died, but none of us heard what he said. How dry his mouth must have been after all those hours on the cross.

When they were sure he was dead, the Roman soldiers lowered the cross to the ground. They were surprisingly gentle. A man we didn't know arrived with a cart pulled by two servants and had them place my brother's body on the cart. He sent them down the road Jesus had come up just that morning. Then the man asked the soldier a question, and he gestured toward us. The man came to where we stood waiting, not knowing what to do next.

"I am Joseph of Arimathaea," he introduced himself. "I am a member of the Council, but I dissented in the voting. He didn't need to die. I have a tomb where we can lay him. It is a safe place for his body until you can prepare it for burial day after next. You won't have time today, as sunset is fast approaching and the Sabbath soon begins."

I thanked Joseph, and we followed him to the tomb where we watched Jesus' body laid inside. The men who had pulled the cart rolled a giant rock over the entrance. Numbly, we watched, then we went home before the sun set.

The next day my mother did not rise from her bed at all. I fed her broth, but we did not talk and I did not urge her to get up. She seemed shrunken, and her characteristic vitality was gone. 'I'll lose her next,' I thought, 'and my father will not be far behind. How does one survive such losses?'

The men came back into Jerusalem, sick with their own loss. Peter, usually large and bluff, seemed subdued, smaller. Little by little he told us how he had denied Jesus. Though I could see he was in agony over his betrayal, equating it nearly with that of

Judas, I could find nothing to say to ease his guilt.

None of us could comfort each other. We were locked in small cells of individual grief. We barely spoke. We even avoided touch on this day after Jesus' crucifixion, as if we would easily bruise or break. The community was fragmented into individuals, each with our own burdens and our own feelings, which we were unable to share.

I found myself riding an ebb and flow of anger and grief. I had feelings I'd never had before. I wanted to kill somebody, make somebody pay for my brother's death. I felt the vision had betrayed us, YHWH had betrayed us.

I didn't know who I was without Jesus. We had been together even in our mother's womb. All our lives we had been part of each other, which meant part of me was in that tomb with my brother. I needed an accounting. I couldn't suffer this without a reason, but there could never be a reason good enough to explain the death of my brother.

All my memories were torturing me, the same memories that would later bring me joy. I could almost smell the rich wood smells of our father's shop, picture the River Jordan, where John swore he heard the voice of the Lord anointing Jesus. I thought of the many campfires we had built, the many lives we had touched. Was that all gone with him? What would I do now? How could any of us go on without Jesus?

CHAPTER TWENTY-TWO

We rested on the Sabbath, then rose early the first day of the week to go to the tomb, myself, Joanna, Mary of Magdala, and Mary the mother of James. My mother still lay in bed, weak and too ill to rise. I fully expected her to die of a broken heart.

We had prepared ointments to anoint Jesus' body for a proper burial. We wanted to do what was right, but we were a sad and quiet lot, our spirits downtrodden. The very way we walked, bent over, our faces toward the ground, signaled our despair and emptiness as we came upon the tomb loaned to us by Joseph of Arimathaea. We were a little surprised to see the stone rolled away from the door of the tomb, but thought the workmen had come before us and not waited. Joanna and I, in the lead, ran to the tomb and peered into the dim interior. The slab upon which Jesus' body had been laid was empty.

I believe it was Joanna who screamed, though it might have been me. This was the one thing too many, the one unbearable thing of all the unbearable happenings. To have lost our beloved from our midst, and now his body as well . . . it could not be borne.

The two Marys came up behind us. Mary of Magdala, seeing the empty tomb, slid to the ground before any of us could react. Joanna and Mary and I gathered her up. As soon as I touched her, I knew that she was only faint, not dead, and she began to come around immediately.

As we helped her up, two beings in dazzling white garments, very like the angels Jesus and I had dreamed about, appeared at our side. They spoke to us.

"Why search here for one who is alive? Remember how he told you, while he was still in Galilee, that he must be given into the power of sinful men and be crucified, and would rise again on the third day?" So saying, they were gone as inexplicably as they had appeared.

The four of us turned to each other. We remembered what Jesus had said, but we had trouble connecting it to what was happening right then. Who were these beings? Who sent them? What was it they were trying to tell us? And why us? We were just women. Why not tell Peter or one of the other disciples? Did they mean that Jesus had been resurrected? How could that be? What did it mean? What should we tell people?

Finally, getting ourselves back together, we returned to the house where the eleven were staying and told them exactly what we saw and heard. The story appeared to them to be nonsense, and they did not believe us. Actually, we were not sure what to believe ourselves, so the disciples' reaction did not upset us.

We spent some time talking over possibilities, deciding to get in touch with Joseph of Arimathaea as soon as possible to see if he had moved the body for some reason. Our illusion, delusion, or vision could be accounted for by our grief and our exhaustion. We all felt that the last months spent moving inexorably toward Jerusalem, the trial, and the crucifixion had robbed us of our energy and our hope. No wonder we thought we saw angels, especially ones who promised that Jesus was not dead.

It was decided that Philip and James would try to find Joseph, while Joanna and Mary the mother of James left for their homes. The streets were unusually quiet, as if Jerusalem were ashamed of herself. Even the marketplace, where we stopped to get food for the noon meal, was subdued, so it did not take us long. None of us was very hungry.

It happened as Mary of Magdala and I neared the house where we were staying. Jesus appeared beside me, walking along with me as we had walked countless times in our lives. It seemed so natural that my feelings were delayed and, by the time I would have shouted, whether in fear or joy, he spoke.

"Don't be afraid, D'vorah, for it is truly me."

The two of us stopped and gathered around him. Mary

moved into his arms as if it were the most natural thing, and I could tell by the way he held her that this was no dream, no delusion, but Jesus himself who was with us. The crucifixion, that terrible day on Golgotha, suddenly seemed an aberration we could put behind us.

As if reading our minds, Jesus said, "Yes, I am real and alive, but what you witnessed on Golgotha was as real as this."

He held out his hands where the wounds showed, angry and inflamed. Mary, suddenly alert, stepped back from him, fear on her small, dear face. He turned to her and gently put one arm back around her and drew her close again.

"Fear not, Mary. Though I was crucified, I have been resurrected. You," he gestured toward us all, "are my witnesses. You watched while I died, and you see me here today. It will be partly up to you to carry our message out into the world, and you can tell them that I have transcended death. It is the proof you will need to show the world there is another way to live."

He took me under his other arm. I flinched from his side, remembering the great wound there, but he pulled me firmly to him. He felt as solid as ever to me, and I could feel my heart beating to match his.

"D'vorah," he spoke with great calm, "you, Mary, and our mother are the three I love the best. Ease your hearts with the knowledge that I have not died for nothing, but like the prophets of old, and John before me, my death has meaning beyond our understanding."

Gently, he kissed Mary, then me. And with that he was gone from us.

There were many who saw Jesus after we did. He appeared to our mother and brought her comfort so that she grew strong again. The disciples saw him, as did most of the community, even those who had gone away before we came up to Jerusalem. He appeared where people were; they did not have to go looking for him. And he promised baptism with the Holy Spirit and a role in establishing the Kingdom. After a time he came no more, and some said that he was lifted up into the clouds, out of our sight.

I never saw him again, nor did Mary of Magdala, but we knew that he had somehow cheated death. It did not stop us from missing him, but it cut our loss by half to know that death did not have the final say.

CHAPTER TWENTY-THREE

As soon as Mother was well enough, she and I went home. Father looked much older than I remembered, very bony and fragile, but my younger sisters had taken good care of him. Even so, he was glad and relieved to see Mother, who promised never to leave him again. She was as good as her promise, and he died quietly in his sleep three weeks after her return.

The news about Jesus' death had arrived home before we did. Already the story of his resurrection had been embellished, and there were those who wanted to know all about it, as well as those who began avoiding members of my family. It didn't take long to sort out who was who.

Many of those who came to talk to me and my mother were attracted by the sensational stories. If we had the time, we usually sat with them and told what we knew. I talked about the years we had wandered, and Mother told about the last days. Together our stories amounted to what we knew to be the truth as we had lived it.

For some, this wasn't enough. They loved what they called the miracles, the healing and feeding the crowds, but didn't want to know that Jesus had also been an ordinary man with extraordinary gifts. Neither did they want to hear my part in it. There was no place in their understanding of things for a woman who had participated in her brother's ministry. These people left disappointed, I'm afraid.

For others, our very words formed a lifeline, saving them from lives of hopelessness and despair. They hungered for our message, longed for our vision of the new world where they would have an exalted place. But they did not want to hear my part in it either, except for some of the women, who listened silently and intently.

Thus it was that I developed a second version of the story, with Jesus at the center. I ascribed my healings to him, my thoughts to him, my own particular understanding of things to him. The fact that no one questioned how Jesus would have known the things he knew, done the things he did, especially the healing of women and children, proved to me that I was right in re-working the truth. It was the message that counted, I told myself. It was a decision I lived to regret.

We found that the people who avoided us wanted no contact with Jesus, the heretic. These were good people, for the most part, whose whole way of life, their values and their religion, had been challenged by Jesus of Nazareth, by what he taught, by his very person. He had set himself up as a false Messiah, they felt, and therefore they stayed at a great distance from his family and friends. I never questioned their judgment. Our beliefs already had a high enough cost.

I thought that the community would break up once Jesus, who was its focus, was gone, but I was wrong. The disciples stayed together after the crucifixion and were visited by the Holy Spirit, as Jesus had promised. I received a letter from Peter, dictated to a scribe, telling how tongues of fire filled with the Holy Spirit rested on each of them, and how they had all talked in languages they did not know but could understand, nevertheless.

"We have made many converts, D'vorah," Peter wrote, "and, though we have been forbidden to speak, we continue to tell of Jesus' death and resurrection. Those who believe repent and are baptized.

"The community grows," the letter continued, "and we need you to come to us. Many of the converts are women, and though Joanna, the Marys, and Martha are very good with them, we all miss you and wish you were here with us. Won't you come?"

I will admit I was tempted, but I was afraid to leave my mother. Then the news reached me, after my father's death, that

Peter and John had been brought repeatedly to court and were in some danger of being imprisoned. Mother and I packed up once again, leaving my sisters and brothers and their families to guard our interests as well as their own, and joined a pack train to Jerusalem.

CHAPTER TWENTY-FOUR

We arrived back in Jerusalem, some months after we left, to find the community growing and very well organized. Many people with some wealth, property, and personal goods had joined, and what they had was redistributed to those in need. In this way no one in our community went without the necessary things in life, just as Jesus and I had envisioned. But it brought to mind the endless troubles over food we had once had. It was wonderful to see that food was no longer hoarded and no one went hungry. My mother and I were welcomed by all, those with whom we had shared so much, as well as the new people.

Mary of Magdala, who had grown plumper, seemed so at ease with herself and others. She regularly preached to the assembly about the Kingdom, which had come true for her in Jesus, and had a regular ministry of her own with women possessed by the many demons that had plagued her. The demons knew enough to fear her power and would flee at the mention of Jesus' name. In this way Mary brought many women into the community.

Martha and Mary had sold their house and worldly goods to live with the community in Jerusalem. Martha's organizational skills were greatly appreciated in this large group. Mary taught motherless young girls about Jesus and about what it meant to be a woman in the Kingdom. The same gentle stillness that had so aggravated her sister helped these girls to trust Mary and to practice the things she taught.

My first thought, after I grew accustomed to the great numbers of people, was how much Jesus would have enjoyed and approved of the community. It resembled nothing so much as the new order of our vision, and Mother and I rejoiced in it. At the Sabbath meals we remembered Jesus' life, death, and resurrection in the ritual of breaking bread. The memorial came to mean a great deal to me.

It was not long before we were called upon to tell our stories to the community, and I heard, for the first time, exactly how much Mother knew before our birth just what Jesus' life would be like. She knew about the healing power and, unknown to us, had helped us keep it a secret for so many years. She knew about the three years we had wandered. She knew about the inevitability of the crucifixion, as she told us before we went up to Jerusalem. That was why she and Father never stood in our way. It solved an ancient riddle for me, while creating a new one. She never told me the source of her knowledge.

Soon after we arrived, the apostles were arrested by the Sadducean party and imprisoned. The morning after they were imprisoned, daybreak found them teaching in The Temple. It seems an angel of the Lord had opened their prison doors.

They were quickly taken into custody again and brought before the Council, who warned them once more to cease preaching in Jesus' name. Peter told the Council that the apostles must obey the Lord rather than men, and that Jesus had been raised up at the Lord's right hand as leader and savior to grant Israel repentance and forgiveness of sins.

I would have liked to have seen their faces when Peter said that. This hardly seemed the same man who had denied Jesus thrice on the day of the crucifixion. It raised such fury in the Council that they wanted to have all the apostles put to death, and only the intervention of a Pharisee called Gamaliel stopped them. He reminded the Council of other men who had made claims to the throne of Israel but whose movements had broken up on their own, and suggested that the Council let this new movement do the same. The apostles were flogged and went directly back to preaching the good news of Jesus.

The workings of the community were not without flaws. The apostles established a system whereby those who disagreed could get together with others who had no vested interest in the dispute and talk until things had been worked out. This had to be done incident by incident, as the population of the community was always in flux. For instance, the Greek-speaking people brought a complaint against those who spoke the language of the Jews, that their widows were being overlooked in the daily distribution. This resulted in the appointment of seven men of good repute to oversee the distribution of goods.

I had noticed Stephen, one of these seven, months before when we had first returned to Jerusalem. He had joined the community soon after the resurrection and, though I thought I had given up any thoughts of marriage long ago, my eyes always wandered to him in any group, and I found myself near him at table and on many other occasions. We quickly moved from mere acquaintance toward friendship.

He was somewhat younger than I. His hair had gold in it, and his eyes were the color of honey. He had been married, but his wife had died in childbirth, leaving him to raise his child, a daughter, just turned ten. I liked his soft-spoken ways and his kindness, not only toward his daughter but also toward everyone else in the community. He compared well with my brother. It was not long before Stephen was regarded by all as a man of faith, though my interest in him was more than that, to my surprise.

Stephen fell afoul of the Council when it was alleged that he had made blasphemous statements against Moses and against YHWH. I was in court the day he appeared. I could not stay away. It was obvious from the beginning that Stephen had been set up, so nothing he said helped, though he gave a brilliant history of our people, especially our troubled relationship with God.

"You are so stubborn," he ended his impassioned speech, "heathen at heart and deaf to the truth! You always resist. You are just like your fathers! Was there ever a prophet your fathers did not persecute? They killed those who foretold the coming of the Messiah, and now you have betrayed him and killed him. You received the law given by God, and yet you have not kept it."

I sat with members of our community, and we held our breath as Stephen launched a full-out attack on his captors. He held nothing back, risked all, proclaiming that Jesus stood at God's right hand. I willed him to be silent. Our friendship was just beginning, and I wanted to know where it might go. I was already fond of his daughter. Could this be what I had missed, come to me late in my life, the love of a good man, a daughter of my own?

"Oh, Stephen," I willed, "say no more. Let them have their way so that we might have a life."

But it was too late. He had gone too far. They told me later about the stoning. Later, after I returned to be with Lois, his daughter, they told me — and I told her — how her father had called out, the last stones crashing into his bloody, beaten body, "Lord Jesus, receive me."

They told me — and I told her — how he had cried, as he fell, "Do not hold this sin against them."

CHAPTER TWENTY-FIVE

Stephen's death was nearly too much for me, but I kept up appearances for Lois' sake. The girl was now without any family of her own. She gravitated to me as her father's friend, and I must admit that it was because of her that I was able to continue with my work. I took her with me when I went to preach or just to meet with groups of women, and she began an apprenticeship with Mary of Magdala in the healing arts.

She was sweet and shy and reminded me in many ways of her father. Her faith in the new way was also reflective of his, and she told me many times that Stephen was now with Jesus and that we would join them when our time came. In my darker moments I hoped she was right. She seemed to have no doubts or regrets about the path she was on, though her father had died for it. It was good for me to be around her, and I knew she was a special gift.

My mother died quite suddenly, not long after Stephen's death. Though she was old and would have been glad for the quick way that she died, I was distraught. Peter reminded me that, over time, I would come to myself again, and the grief would be replaced by a gentle melancholy as I got back to the business my life was about. I didn't appreciate his reminder, even though I knew it to be true. So, Mary of Magdala and I held each other and wept for my mother, whom I miss to this day, as I miss my brother. The grief may ebb, but the sense of loss never entirely goes away.

More and more women, in addition to the many men, entered our community as the years passed, and they loved to hear the stories of how Jesus and I began. Over the years my memory of those long ago days did not fade but remained brightly lit in my heart, always ready to be told to anyone who wanted to hear. I repeated many of the conversations Jesus and I had had with each other and with John the Baptizer, and the women would pick up the threads of the stories, weave them with their own, as the web of women's stories grew and grew.

Each woman found a special place in the community, and not only the traditional woman's place. Quite a few were gifted speakers and traveled with some of the men, establishing small communities throughout the land. It seemed the women were less worried about the persecution of our communities than many of the men. They had very little to lose, they told me.

Many of them proved to be healers of different kinds. These were referred to me, and we became known for our knowledge and skill. Some knew about herbs, some knew how to set bones and stitch up wounds. I could still heal through touch, though it took more out of me every year.

Even though we added members to our community every day and our internal workings were largely smooth, we were subjected to increasing persecution from without. One of those present at the stoning of Stephen, Saul of Tarsus, was particularly virulent in his attacks on us, and he traveled the length and breadth of the land to arrest followers of the new way. His name became synonymous with danger.

For this reason, when rumors came from Damascus that Saul had been converted to our way and renamed Paul, the community remained skeptical and on guard. The arrival of the disciple Ananias from Damascus with the full story of the conversion and all that followed could scarcely be credited.

He reported that Saul had been traveling to Damascus to get authorization from the synagogue to arrest our followers when a great light had flashed around him and a voice had boomed from the sky: "Saul, Saul, why are you persecuting my people?"

"Who are you?" Saul had asked.

"I am Jesus," the voice had answered. "Get up and go into the city. You will be told what to do."

When Saul got up, he was blind. The men he was traveling with had not seen the light, but they had heard the voice, so they took Saul to Damascus where he fasted for three days.

Ananias, meantime, had a vision wherein he was instructed to go to Saul and heal his blindness by touching him, which he did, even though he knew Saul to be an enemy of our people. Saul's blindness healed, he was baptized, and he ate until his strength returned. Later, he preached about Jesus in the synagogue and was met with great skepticism. Someone disliked his preaching enough to organize an attempt on his life, which, like other attempts, he escaped.

Saul, an educated man of middle years, had made it his life's work to destroy the Jesus movement. Following his experience on the road to Damascus and his healing by Ananias, he gave himself, as Paul, with the same amount of zeal, entirely to the movement's growth.

He began to institute a variety of changes in the community, out of his personal understanding of what was needed in the world, I am sure. With Peter, he changed the dietary laws that were fixed in Judaism and baptized the uncircumcised. I wondered at the time what Jesus would have thought. I wasn't sure what I thought myself.

Both these actions were heretical and brought more trouble to us, but, at the same time, many non-Jews joined our community. Meetings in private houses, some with women at their heads, were established in many places. Some of them were quite large and very active in recruiting converts. Separately and together Peter, Jesus' stalwart, and the convert Paul carried the word of the new way to the Gentiles in Judea and Samaria. Paul's letters to the far-flung and persecuted congregations held them together and addressed problems the growing community faced. He became in every way the center of the new religion.

CHAPTER TWENTY-SIX

I am now very old, and my life and usefulness are approaching an end. But, still, so many years later, I remember everything that happened. What is most remarkable to me is how little of the work that Jesus and I actually did is recalled by our own people today. Oh, some of the stories told, father to son, mother to daughter, resemble what I remember. There is even some talk now of writing the stories down, though that would not be safe for us at this time.

I go around, as I am able, to be with the community at table and when they gather together to tell the stories, so I know what they are saying. I have very little importance to most of these people, which bothers me not at all. I have spent most of my life being overlooked. I am asked to heal from time to time, when someone realizes who I am. The healing, though, takes more from me than I care, sometimes, to give. Still, it seems selfish to with-hold such a gift, now that I and Mary of Magdala are the only ones left to have it.

Peter is gone from us, along with most of the others. Lois, who is grown, believes they are with Jesus, her father, and the rest. It comforts her. The apostles healed, too, after Jesus' death, but I think it frightened them. I half believe that Jesus, wherever he is now, loaned them the power to see if they could use it and, finding that it upset them, withdrew it after a time.

No one ever asks me what I think about Paul and what he is doing in my brother's name. Perhaps they think I am too old to think anything or that what I think doesn't matter. Well, I am not too old, but it doesn't matter what I think. It is just as Jesus and I said it would be. They are building the community they want, not the new world we envisioned. It does resemble more and more what we wished to change, so I try not to be too disappointed.

The stories that are being passed down through the community surprise me because of what has already been forgotten, though some of it may be my own fault. Jesus and I walked the length and breadth of this land for three years. He preached mainly outdoors, while I talked with the women in their homes. Everywhere we went, we told of our vision for the future: a land without war, a people whole and undivided, equality and liberation for all, a heaven here on earth, today, in our time, as well as in the afterlife. Everywhere we went, we healed. Demons were cast out, marriages were repaired, the blind were given sight, adulterers were brought back to YHWH, the lame walked, children were cured of fits.

We worked together but in differing ways, as befitted our accustomed roles. Jesus worked largely in public, while I worked largely in private. Although we worked together many times, as in the instance of Jairus' daughter, I have now been dropped from the story, though I have long outlived my brother and continued active in the community. It is with profound regret that I remember blending our stories for eager listeners. I would have done well to tell only the truth, be it believed or not. The truth would have better served our vision than the altered stories do.

And so many of the women's stories are no more, except in my own bright, clear memory. The Marys: my own sweet mother, the one from Bethany, and Jesus' companion, the Magdalene, have all become one and lost their individual identities. Naomi, Rebecca, Sarah, Tamar, and Esther are now as if they never were.

Where, I wonder, have their stories gone? Tamar, for instance, who was beaten and repeatedly raped by Roman soldiers until, when she was brought to me, she was still and vacant within herself, her soul gone from her body. Where is the story of her recovery, of her return to wholeness as I held her for hours, the power pouring through me, as I urged her to rage against injustice, not to give herself up to it? Tamar, who not only recovered but later often walked with women after dark so they would not be alone when the soldiers were drinking and loose in the town. No woman who walked with Tamar was ever assaulted. Where is her story?

And where is Rebecca's story? Rebecca, who tried to leave her husband because he ravaged their tiny daughter. Rebecca, who brought the torn and bleeding infant to me in the dead of night. I could have healed the child and comforted the woman, but the father found us together and violently accused me of ruining his family and leading his badly frightened wife astray. Only by sending for Jesus was I able to stave off a very dangerous situation, and together we healed not only the child but the wife and husband as well. Where is this story of a family in which all had to be made whole?

Mine has been a long life, much longer than is right, really. I have outlived everyone who was there when Jesus was crucified, and I alone am left to try to tell the stories only I remember. But many of the stories are being told as people wish, not as things really happened. Jesus and I will be remembered not for who we were but for what people need us to be. Still, it hurts me to think that our beautiful, strange, and frightening lives, and the lives of those who walked with us, will not be faithfully recalled, even by those who claim to love us.

Our mother will not be remembered for her strength and wisdom and the beauty of all her children, but for her eldest son only. Mary Magdalene, Jesus' beloved, will not be remembered as his true companion and carrier of his message after his death, but as one of several Marys. The sisters, Martha and Mary, along with the rest of the women, have already been dropped from the story of the Passover meal that so many of us shared as Jesus neared his death. In the midst of travail, we celebrated our lives and works, yet, in the story that is now being told, Jesus was alone with the twelve. Who, I wonder every time I hear this rendition, cooked, served, and cleaned up? Even men who should know better seem to believe that the meal simply appeared to Jesus and the twelve.

At least it is remembered that we went to Calvary with him, the other women and I, though we are largely nameless. While the men scattered far and wide in their confusion and fear, we were there at the foot of the cross. Later, we were at the tomb — for Jesus, and for ourselves. Oh, how we wept in each other's arms in the days that followed for all the losses of our women's lives: the children who died in infancy or childhood; the husbands, fathers, and brothers maimed and murdered by the Romans; the sisters dead in childbirth or from hunger and a thousand kinds of illness. We wept until we were empty vessels, and then we did what women have always done: We put ourselves back together and went about the work that was before us to do.

Thus it is I have lived. As I near the end, I only wish the women who come after me can learn from my having lived as I have that they do not need to stay within the narrow boundaries set for them. It is true that Jesus and I were given great gifts, and that we tried to use them well and for the benefit of those we knew or met. It is true that we lived in extraordinary times and that I have seen in my lifetime much change. Even so, we were often filled with very human doubts and despair.

Our gifts, which set us apart from others, called for great discernment and courage, but we were willing to take the necessary risks. For Jesus, because he was a man, they led to his death. Only I, Jesus' twin, a woman, am left to tell that it is possible, even for women, to live lives that are far from ordinary and to use for good the gifts each one of us has in abundance and diversity. If my life can serve as encouragement to women who follow after me to take the risks their lives call for, then I will consider it well lived, as I go at last to join my brother, my parents, Stephen, and all who have gone before in the hereafter of equals we envisioned all our lives.

EPILOGUE
Author's Commentary

Chapter 1: The version of the story of Jesus' birth with which we, in this culture, are most familiar is told in Luke. It was in Luke's version that there was "no room at the inn," and Jesus was born in a stable and placed in a manger. See Luke 2:1-20.

Chapter 2: Though I did not refer precisely to Jesus' comments on little children, this description is what I had in mind, in terms of his patience with his little sisters and brothers. See Matthew 19:13-15, Mark 10:13-16, Luke 18:15-17, John 3:3, 5.

Chapter 3: The story of Mary's cousin Elizabeth, mother of John the Baptist, is exclusive to Luke. John's birth is the precursor of Jesus' birth, as John's ministry points to Jesus' ministry. See Luke 1:5-80.

Chapter 4: I deliberately did not debate the veracity of the miraculous healings found throughout the New Testament, but based inferences about the possibility of D'vorah's unrecognized divinity on her full sharing of this gift.

Chapter 5: Jesus' visit to The Temple and being left behind in Jerusalem is also peculiar to Luke (2:41-52).

Chapter 6: If one accepts Jesus' humanity, whether as a part of his divinity, or alone, how he came to hold his radical views needs to be told in the context of his relationships. There are enough reports in the Christian Bible of Jesus' unorthodox encounters with women and his conversations with them on many subjects, that I believe such conversations as these between D'vorah and Jesus are not implausible. Jesus did not become who he was in a vacuum. Rather, as do all of us, he grew to adulthood in a family and a community that would have put their mark on his beliefs.

Chapters 7 & 8: D'vorah, as Jesus' twin, like him in all ways but gender, stood in a different place in her culture than did her brother. Though I think we sometimes believe that women's conscious awareness of their own separateness and oppression is a modern phenomenon, I believe that women in all oppressive cultures know they are oppressed, even without our sophisticated language to describe their condition. I also believe that our historic sisters, as women still must often do, formed a female community within the larger community, an underground, a survival and support system, which allowed them to endure life as property, as subhumans, and to find enough meaning to go on.

Chapter 9: I added this story to establish D'vorah as an autonomous person.

Chapter 10: Jesus' baptism by his cousin is central to the recognition of his divinity in the Synoptic Gospels. See Matthew 3:1-17, Mark 1:1-11, Luke 3:1-18, 21-22.

Chapter 11: I used the temptation of Jesus by the Devil to mark the point at which Jesus knew that he must make himself visible to the world and take D'vorah with him. As in other instances, I did not concentrate on Jesus' oft-told story, but on the women's untold stories through D'vorah's narrative. See Matthew 4:1-11, Mark 1:12-13, Luke 4:1-13.

Chapter 12: The Beatitudes in Matthew and Luke, and some of the following text in Luke, may be some of the most radical religious teachings ever spoken. It is primarily these messages of hope and love that I had in mind as I thought and wrote about Jesus and D'vorah. See Matthew 5:3-12 and Luke 6:20-22, 27-36, 37-42.

Chapter 13: In my re-telling of the Jesus story, this is the first public and visible healing by Jesus and D'vorah. See Matthew 7:28-29, Mark 1:21-28, Luke 4:31-37, John 7:46.

Chapter 14: The healing of Peter's mother-in-law is told in Matthew 8:14-17, Mark 29:34, Luke 4:38-41.

Chapter 15: Jesus eats with sinners and tax collectors in Matthew 9:9-13, Mark 2:1-12, Luke 5:17-26. Jesus heals on the Sabbath in Matthew 12:9-14, Mark 3:1-6, Luke 6:6-11. The healing of the woman with a flow of blood, which occurs within the story of the healing of Jairus' daughter, happens only in the Synoptic Gospels and is similar in all three, Matthew 9:18-26, Mark 5:21-43, and Luke 8:40-56. It is an interesting story because it indicates an exchange of a powerful sort taking place between Jesus and those he healed. The encounter is not one-way, but circular between the two of them, and Jesus knows this. The parable of the yeast is in Matthew 13:33 and Luke 13:20. The woman with the lost coins is only in Luke 15:8-10. The Golden Rule is in Matthew 7:12, and I pulled my paraphrased text from Luke 6:27-31. There is no comparable text in Mark, the earliest source.

Chapter 16: Much has been written about the woman who anoints Jesus with priceless oil or ointment. Some say she was Mary of Bethany, where the scene is placed in Matthew 26:6-13 and Mark 14:3-9. It is from this text that eminent theologian Elisabeth Schussler Fiorenza pulled the title of her book *In Memory of Her*, though this nameless woman and her prophetic anointment of Jesus' head with oil has long since been diminished in importance by Christian tradition. John's Gospel identifies her as the sister of Martha and Lazarus (John 11:1-2). In Luke 7:36-50, the city is not named, the woman is a sinner, and she anoints Jesus' feet with ointment. In this later version of the text, Jesus uses the incident as an opportunity to lecture his followers about great love and faith, and forgives her sins.

Chapter 17: There is no one in the Bible, save Jesus and his mother, about which more has been spoken and written than Mary Magdalene. In Christian tradition she has become a prostitute, though in the Gospels she is never so called, and there are very few mentions of her except as one of the female followers out of whom Jesus cast seven devils (Luke 8:1-3). Some have called Mary Jesus' "companion," and in some of the Gnostic and later Protestant traditions she is seen to have been very close to him during his ministry. Some people feel that the woman taken in adultery (John 8:1-11) may have been Mary.

John's imprisonment and the story of his death can be found only in Matthew 14:3-12 and Mark 16:17-29. The parallel stories of the feeding of the multitudes are to be found in Matthew 14:13-21 and 15:32-39, Mark 6:30-44 and 8:1-10. Only the first feeding of the five thousand is to be found in Luke (9:10-17).

Chapter 18: The stories of the sisters Martha and Mary are found in Luke 10:38-42, John 11:1-3. As an interesting note, in John, which breaks from the Synoptic Gospels in both tone and content, Martha chastises Jesus that he did not come to her brother Lazarus before he died. In one of the most compelling scenes of this late Gospel, she tells him that he could have saved her brother (John 11:21-22). For me, that scene, with Martha blaming Jesus for letting her brother die, illuminates the equity that existed between Jesus and the women in his circle. Martha is not afraid of Jesus, nor in awe of him, though she understands very well the extent of his power, and he does go on to raise her brother from the dead. The story of Lazarus is to be found only in John 10:40-11:44. This story is one of the few in which Jesus weeps and shows human emotion.

Jesus heals a woman who has been bent over double for eighteen years in Luke 13:10-17, on the Sabbath, which was forbidden. In so many of his actions, many relating to women who were considered by other men to be property, Jesus stepped outside his tradition and broke the societal laws governing behavior.

Chapter 19: This chapter is my personal statement about the nature of right action or ethical living. Particularly in times as complex as ours, I believe it is necessary to understand that we do not need to believe our goals will be reached in order to continue working for needed change, but that the nature of faith has more to do with the intrinsic goodness of acting well and rightly, even in the face of hopelessness.

It is also in this chapter that I deliberately sidestepped the issue of Jesus' divinity and his own belief about whether or not he was the Messiah. Because the story works all ways, with a divine Jesus, a specially gifted human-healer Jesus, or a mere mortal man about whom extraordinary things happened, I left it alone. The Jesus story has survived through time because of the message the story carries, even with its different interpretations. I am personally more interested in the message, as I interpret it, than in a lengthy discussion of what may constitute divinity.

In this chapter I also refer to stories of some of the other nameless women: the Samaritan woman (John 4:4-42), and the Canaanite (Matthew 15:21-28) or Syrophoenician (Mark 7:24-30) woman.

Chapter 20: Jesus' entry into Jerusalem, as recounted in the biblical stories, is necessary, as so much else in the Gospels, to fix the fulfillment of prophecy (Matthew 21:1-17, Mark 11:1-11, Luke 19:28-46, John 12:12-50). When Jesus drives the money changers out of The Temple, the tempo, as the story approaches the crucifixion, hastens (Matthew 21:12-13, Mark 11:15-19, Luke 19:45-48, John 2:13-17).

I have never understood how the Passover/Seder dinner, known in Christian tradition as the Last Supper, could be represented as having included only Jesus and the twelve disciples. Given the fact that women traveled with Jesus, were part of his ministry, were the first to know who he truly was, and stood by him to the last, their elimination at this crucial juncture seems a cruel oversight (Matthew 26:17-19, 26:26-29; Mark 14:12-16, 22-25; Luke 22:7-13, 15-20).

Judas' betrayal and Jesus' capture are told in Matthew 26:47-56, Mark 14:43-52, Luke 22:47-53, and John 18:2-12, 20.

Chapter 21: Each version of the crucifixion, especially in reference to Jesus' death, is slightly different. The best known version is that in which Jesus asks God (ABBA="Father") to forgive his killers. This is the story told in Luke 23:34. In John, Jesus gives his mother over into the care of an unnamed disciple (19:25-27), believed in the tradition to be the Gospel writer John, though none of the disciples is reported near the cross at the time of Jesus' death in any of the earlier Synoptic Gospels. In Matthew 27:45-61 and Mark 15:33-47, the women watch from afar, and Jesus asks his Father, God, why he has been forsaken.

Joseph of Arimathaea takes responsibility for Jesus' burial in all four Gospels: Matthew 27:57-61, Mark 15:42-47, Luke 23:50-56, and John 19:38-42.

Peter's denial of Jesus (Matthew 26:69-75, Mark 15:66-72, Luke 22:54-62, John 18:15-18, 25-27) seems to me to indicate the terror the disciples had of the world without Jesus. Throughout the stories, their faith is slender, more wishful thinking than anything, though the women see Jesus clearly and, if the narratives are to be believed, never doubt him. I do not wish to cast this in a hierarchical mode, that the women are better than the men, because that is not what I believe. What I do believe is that the women, as marginalized people, had much to gain by believing Jesus, while most of the men, holders and inheritors of traditional modes of power, had much to lose. It is the diverse places in which these two groups of people stand that must account for the differences in what they see and are able to grasp about Jesus.

Chapter 22: The women's discovery of the empty tomb is reported in all the Gospels. In Matthew 28:1-10, Mary Magdalene and the other Mary go to the tomb, where they are greeted by an earthquake and an angel, then by Jesus himself as they are returning to the disciples. In Mark 16:1-8, the women are Mary Magdalene, Mary the mother of James, and Salome. A young man in the empty tomb tells them Jesus has risen. In the shorter ending, they are afraid and tell no one. In the longer ending, Mary Magdalene sees Jesus and tells the disciples, but they do not believe her. In Luke 24:1-12, the women are Mary Magdalene, Joanna, Mary the mother of James, and the other women who had come with him from Galilee. They meet two men in "dazzling clothes" who tell them Jesus has risen. They go and tell the eleven, but are not believed until Peter goes to the tomb himself. It is in Luke that Jesus makes many earthly appearances until he is carried up to heaven. In John 20:1-18, Mary Magdalene goes to the tomb alone and, finding it empty, she tells Simon Peter and the nameless disciple "whom Jesus loved" (the same one, no doubt, to whom he gave guardianship of his mother from the cross, possibly John himself). They verify that Jesus is missing and return home. Mary weeps outside the empty tomb, and, in one of the most touching scenes of the Christian Bible, Jesus appears to Mary. Because he makes a point that she not touch him, "because he has not yet ascended," I have grown to believe that she may have been accustomed to touching him before this, that the community may have kissed and embraced in their comings and goings, close friends as they must have been, and that Jesus shared in this physical affection. I feel that this conversation with Jesus must have been enormously comforting to Mary.

Chapter 23: The visitation of the Holy Spirit promised to the disciples by Jesus and the speaking in tongues both occur in Acts 2:1-13.

Chapter 24: The history of the early church, as recounted in The Acts of the Apostles, is believed to be by the same author as Luke's Gospel. Descriptions of the community immediately after Jesus' death are in Acts 1:12-26 and 4:32-37. The apostles are arrested and miraculously freed, rearrested and forbidden to preach, and flogged in Acts 5:17-42. The appointment of the seven to oversee the daily distribution of food is in Acts 6:1-6, and Stephen's story can be found in Acts 6:8-8:1.

Chapter 25: The story of the persecutor of the early Christians, Saul of Tarsus, and his conversion on the road to Damascus, is a paradigm for the true conversion experience (Acts 9:1-19). Paul, as he becomes known, never turns again from his new path, which seems to lead, over time, directly to the formation of the Roman Catholic Church and the systematic conversion of part of the world to Christianity.

Chapter 26: It is my hope I have re-told the stories of the women who followed Jesus with the respect, attention, and love they deserve.

Katherine Schneider-Aker, poet, freelance writer, educator, and activist, devotes her life to helping women rediscover their voices and their power in a variety of ways. In the literary sphere, she not only writes and publishes extensively, but also leads workshops and support groups for other writers. More broadly, she facilitates women's groups for nontraditional woman-based recovery, personal empowerment, and ritual, including work with the California Women's Commission on Alcohol and Drug Dependencies. Katherine is currently enrolled in the Feminist Spirituality master's program at Immaculate Heart College Center, Los Angeles, the city in which she makes her home. A magna cum laude graduate of California State University, Northridge, she is also continuing her studies in their master's program in Creative Writing. A member of the Wild Women Writers, a writers' collective, and the International Women's Writing Guild, she is currently working on a feminist/woman's re-telling of the Arthurian legends, a series of essays on depression in women, and an occasional newsletter.

LuraMedia Publications

BANKSON, MARJORY ZOET
Braided Streams:
Esther and a Woman's Way of Growing
Seasons of Friendship:
Naomi and Ruth as a Pattern
"This Is My Body":
Creativity, Clay, and Change

BOHLER, CAROLYN STAHL
Prayer on Wings: *A Search for Authentic Prayer*

BOZARTH, ALLA RENEE
Womanpriest: *A Personal Odyssey (Rev. Ed.)*

GEIGER, LURA JANE
and **PATRICIA BACKMAN**
Braided Streams Leader's Guide
and **SUSAN TOBIAS**
Seasons of Friendship Leader's Guide

JEVNE, RONNA FAY
It All Begins With Hope:
Patients, Caretakers, and the Bereaved Speak Out
and **ALEXANDER LEVITAN**
No Time for Nonsense:
Getting Well Against the Odds

KEIFFER, ANN
Gift of the Dark Angel: *A Woman's Journey through Depression toward Wholeness*

LODER, TED
Eavesdropping on the Echoes:
Voices from the Old Testament
Guerrillas of Grace:
Prayers for the Battle
No One But Us:
Personal Reflections on Public Sanctuary
Tracks in the Straw:
Tales Spun from the Manger
Wrestling the Light:
Ache and Awe in the Human-Divine Struggle

MEYER, RICHARD C.
One Anothering:
Biblical Building Blocks for Small Groups

MILLETT, CRAIG
In God's Image:
Archetypes of Women in Scripture

O'CONNOR, ELIZABETH
Search for Silence *(Revised Edition)*

PRICE, H.H.
Blackberry Season:
A Time to Mourn, A Time to Heal

RAFFA, JEAN BENEDICT
The Bridge to Wholeness:
A Feminine Alternative to the Hero Myth

SAURO, JOAN
Whole Earth Meditation:
Ecology for the Spirit

SCHAPER, DONNA
A Book of Common Power:
Narratives Against the Current
Stripping Down:
The Art of Spiritual Restoration

WEEMS, RENITA J.
Just a Sister Away: *A Womanist Vision of Women's Relationships in the Bible*

The Women's Series

BORTON, JOAN
Drawing from the Women's Well:
Reflections on the Life Passage of Menopause

CARTLEDGE-HAYES, MARY
To Love Delilah:
Claiming the Women of the Bible

DAHL, JUDY
River of Promise:
Two Women's Story of Love and Adoption

DUERK, JUDITH
Circle of Stones:
Woman's Journey to Herself

O'HALLORAN, SUSAN *and*
DELATTRE, SUSAN
The Woman Who Lost Her Heart:
A Tale of Reawakening

RUPP, JOYCE
The Star in My Heart:
Experiencing Sophia, Inner Wisdom

SCHAPER, DONNA
Superwoman Turns 40:
The Story of One Woman's Intentions to Grow Up

SCHNEIDER-AKER, KATHERINE
God's Forgotten Daughter:
A Modern Midrash — What If Jesus Had Been A Woman?

LuraMedia, Inc. , 7060 Miramar Rd., Suite 104, San Diego, CA 92121
Call 1-800-367-5872 for information about bookstores or ordering.
Books for Healing and Hope, Balance and Justice.